DISCARD

YA   Wilson, David.
951.905
Wil   The Koreas.

CLARK PUBLIC LIBRARY
303 WESTFIELD AVENUE
CLARK, NJ 07066
732-388-5999

Nations in the News
THE KOREAS

Afghanistan

China

India

Iran

The Koreas

Mexico

Russia

Saudi Arabia

Syria

United Kingdom

Nations in the News
 # THE KOREAS

By David Wilson

MASON CREST
Philadelphia · Miami

Mason Crest
450 Parkway Drive, Suite D
Broomall, PA 19008
(866) MCP-BOOK (toll free)
www.masoncrest.com

Copyright © 2020 by Mason Crest, an imprint of National Highlights, Inc. All rights reserved. No part of this publication may be reproduced or transmitted in any form or by any means, electronic or mechanical, including photocopying, recording, taping, or any information storage and retrieval system, without permission in writing from the publisher.

Printed in the United States of America.

First printing
9 8 7 6 5 4 3 2 1

Series ISBN: 978-1-4222-4242-1
Hardcover ISBN: 978-1-4222-4247-6
ebook ISBN: 978-1-4222-7575-7

Cataloging-in-Publication Data is available on file at the Library of Congress.

Developed and Produced by Print Matters Productions, Inc. (www.printmattersinc.com)

Cover and Interior Design by Tom Carling, Carling Design Inc.

QR CODES AND LINKS TO THIRD-PARTY CONTENT
You may gain access to certain third-party content ("third-party sites") by scanning and using the QR Codes that appear in this publication (the "QR Codes"). We do not operate or control in any respect any information, products, or services on such third-party sites linked to by us via the QR Codes included in this publication, and we assume no responsibility for any materials you may access using the QR Codes. Your use of the QR Codes may be subject to terms, limitations, or restrictions set forth in the applicable terms of use or otherwise established by the owners of the third-party sites. Our linking to such third-party sites via the QR Codes does not imply an endorsement or sponsorship of such third-party sites, or the information, products, or services offered on or through the third-party sites, nor does it imply an endorsement or sponsorship of this publication by the owners of such third-party sites.

Contents

Introduction 6
1 Security Issues 18
2 Government and Politics 34
3 Economy 50
4 Quality of Life 66
5 Society and Culture 86
    Series Glossary of Key Terms 100
    Chronology of Key Events 105
    Further Reading & Internet Resources 107
    Index 108
    Author's Biography 111
    Credits 112

KEY ICONS TO LOOK FOR

Words to Understand: These words with their easy-to-understand definitions will increase the reader's understanding of the text while building vocabulary skills.

Sidebars: This boxed material within the main text allows readers to build knowledge, gain insights, explore possibilities, and broaden their perspectives by weaving together additional information to provide realistic and holistic perspectives.

Educational Videos: Readers can view videos by scanning our QR codes, providing them with additional educational content to supplement the text.

Text-Dependent Questions: These questions send the reader back to the text for more careful attention to the evidence presented there.

Research Projects: Readers are pointed toward areas of further inquiry connected to each chapter. Suggestions are provided for projects that encourage deeper research and analysis.

Series Glossary of Key Terms: This back-of-the-book glossary contains terminology used throughout this series. Words found here increase the reader's ability to read and comprehend higher-level books and articles in this field.

A North Korean military parade for the 100th birthday of the late leader Kim Il-sung.

The Koreas at a Glance

Total Land Area	46,489 square miles (North)/38,502 square miles (South)
Climate	Temperate, with rainfall concentrated in summer; long, bitter winters (North and South)
Natural Resources	Coal, iron ore, limestone, magnesite, graphite, copper, zinc, lead, precious metals, hydropower (North) / Coal, tungsten, graphite, molybdenum, lead, hydropower potential (South)
Land Use	Agricultural land: 21.8 percent (19.5 percent arable land, 1.9 percent permanent crops, 0.4 percent permanent pasture); forest: 46 percent; other: 32.2 percent (North)/ Agricultural land: 18.1 percent (15.3 percent arable land, 2.2 percent permanent crops, 0.6 percent permanent pasture); forest: 63.9 percent ; other: 18 percent (South)
Urban Population	61.9 percent of total population (North)/81.5 percent of total population (South)
Major Urban Areas	Pyongyang (3.038 million) (North)/Seoul (9.963 million); Busan (3.467 million); Incheon (2.763 million); Daegu (Taegu) (2.221 million); Daejon (Taejon (1.558 million); Gwangju (Kwangju) (1.518 million) (South)
Geography	Eastern Asia, northern half of the Korean Peninsula bordering the Korean Bay and the Sea of Japan, between China and South Korea; mostly hills and mountains separated by deep, narrow valleys; wide coastal plains in west, discontinuous in east; mountainous interior is isolated and sparsely populated (North)/Eastern Asia, southern half of the Korean Peninsula bordering the Sea of Japan and the Yellow Sea; mostly hills and mountains; wide coastal plains in west and south; about 3,000 mostly small and uninhabited islands off the western and southern coasts (South)

Introduction

North and South Korea may be two of the most different nations in the entire world despite the fact that they share thousands of years of history, language, and culture. The differences between these two nations are between peace and war, democracy and dictatorship, capitalism and **communism**, and freedom and **repression**. These differences define the two nations of North and South Korea, which, despite being fairly small (the 97th and 107th largest in the world, respectively), loom large in ongoing global debates about security, nuclear arms, foreign aid, and human rights. Events that take place in Korea today draw the attention of the entire world.

Relative to 4,000 years of history in Korea, the division between the Communist North and the capitalist South is very new. While Korea has been divided into different kingdoms many times during its history prior to the Korean War of 1950 to 1953, it had never been so rigidly structured into two nations of polar opposites, nor had it ever been so important to the most powerful nations in the

Words to Understand

Communism: An economic and political system where all property is held in common; a form of government in which a one-party state controls the means of production and distribution of resources.

Indoctrinate: To urge assimilation or conformity to a social or political group, sometimes done involuntarily or unconsciously.

Megalopolis: A Greek term meaning "great city," this name is applied to any of the very largest cities or urban areas in the world, usually those with 10 million or more inhabitants.

Repression: Restraining or preventing a population from taking action, by force or the threat of force.

Sanction: An economic (and sometimes military) punishment of a nation that defies international law.

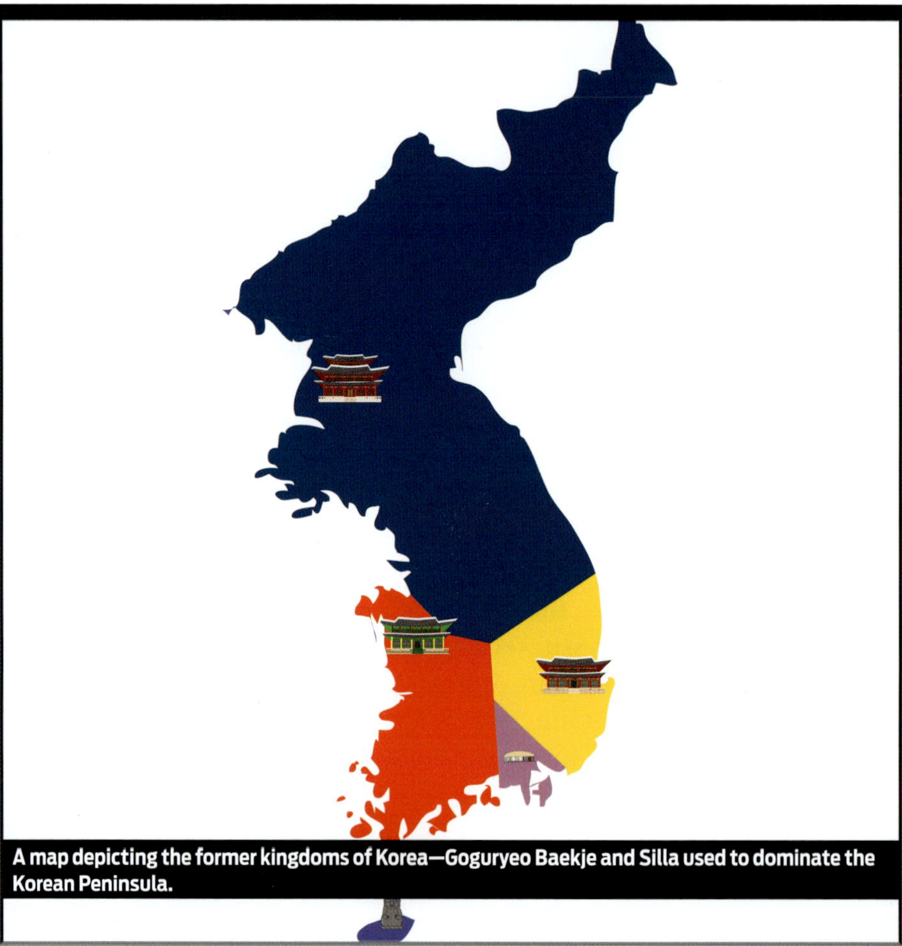

A map depicting the former kingdoms of Korea—Goguryeo Baekje and Silla used to dominate the Korean Peninsula.

world. This conflict, the first hot war of the Cold War, resulted in millions dead and an unhappy division of Korea at the 38th parallel. The North became communist, supported by China and the former Soviet Union, while the South became capitalist, supported by Japan and the United States. This complicated history, coupled with ongoing tensions and strong allies, ensures that Korea often makes global headlines. Furthermore, because the United States has many military bases in South Korea, the region represents a precarious place that countless diplomats, politicians, military leaders, and peace organizations have yet to fully solve.

Nations in the News:  THE KOREAS

The crux of the Korean conflict is that the governments in both North and South Korea refuse to acknowledge the other as legitimate. While neither nation is willing to go to war over this issue (at least, not yet), the risk of tension boiling over into a true conflict has the potential to affect millions of lives. Each nation's alliance is problematic for the other: Relations between South Korea and China are rarely smooth and sometimes contentious, while North Korea has repeatedly demonstrated outright contempt for both Japan and the United States. North Korea's aggressive pursuit of nuclear arms represents a goal that Kim Jong-un and the Communist Party see as the

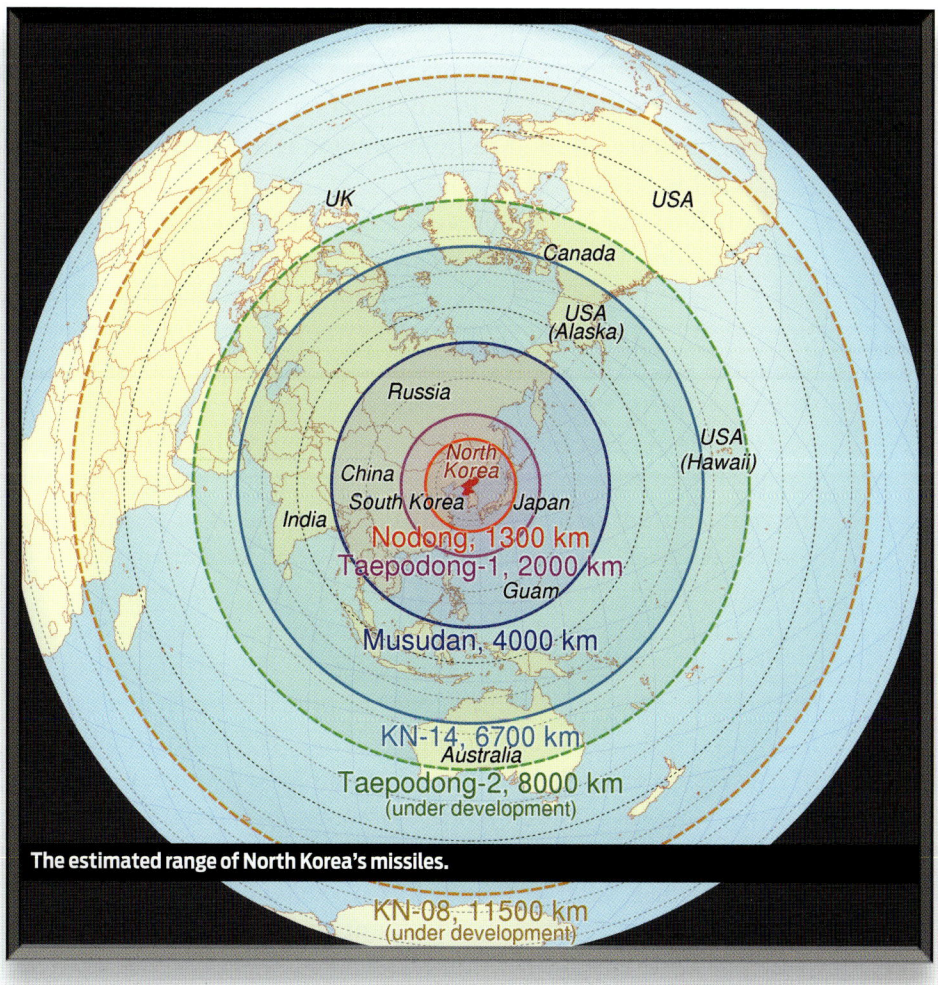

The estimated range of North Korea's missiles.

best way to protect themselves, so much so that they have amended their constitution to make it a national right. The United States and many other nations see North Korea's nuclear program as one of the greatest threats—if not the greatest threat—to world peace.

Attempts to curb North Korea's nuclear program have totally failed at each step. After first withdrawing from the Nuclear Non-Proliferation Treaty in 2003, six-party talks with China, Russia, the United States, Japan, and both Koreas over the span of five years resulted in no progress. Later attempts to put pressure on North Korea through **sanctions** and boycotts nearly crippled the nation's economy yet did not deter North Korean scientists from successful weapons tests. Efforts to bring North Korea to the bargaining table, with both carrots and sticks, have yet to see tangible results. All told, it is clear that the government in Pyongyang puts such a high priority on developing a nuclear weapon that nothing short of full-scale war will deter it. Even if the North Korean people have to eat grass and tree bark, Kim Jong-un will not give up the nuclear weapons his scientists have built.

Many facets of North Korean life might seem incomprehensible to an outsider. Freedoms of speech, political belief, religion, and government criticisms are totally curtailed throughout North Korea. No one, except Kim Jong-un himself, is free to comment on a government that lets its people starve while building billion-dollar nuclear weapons. North Korea **indoctrinates** its people into communism and totalitarianism by promoting an ideology that Kim Jong-un, like his father Kim Jong-il and grandfather Kim Il-sung, is not only the rightful ruler of Korea but also so powerful as to be practically godlike. All North Koreans must work hard on his behalf, expecting virtually nothing in return. Many North Koreans have little idea of a life outside their borders in which people are free to choose their work, their politics, or their words. Access to information is tightly controlled: As but one example, North Korea's Internet gives access to only a few dozen websites, none of which is foreign. Being found in possession of foreign media, information, or political works represents a capital crime in North Korea. Some foreigners who visit North Korea end up in prison without trial or representation for political crimes, such as failure to pay respect to a picture of Kim Jong-un or criticism of his government policies.

Nations in the News:  THE KOREAS

The terrain of the Korean peninsula is mountainous, making farming difficult. Pictured here are the mountains of Seoraksan National Park.

IN THE NEWS

Geography and Culture

Korea's geography has made it somewhat isolated and in turn fostered a unique ethnicity, language, and culture. Its prominence in the world is not a reflection of its geography: Much of the peninsula is mountainous and not practical for cities or farmland; the best farmland in both North and South Korea lies along the narrow coastal plains on the western side of the peninsula. The tallest mountain in Korea is Hallasan, a volcano that stands over 6,000 feet tall on the island of Jeju, sometimes worshipped by Koreans in the belief that spirits reside at its peak. Jeju Island is one of many around both North and South Korea. North and South Korea dispute ownership of some islands, both from one another and from neighboring Russia or Japan. The Taebaek Range forms the backbone of the Korean Peninsula and covers much of the area, leaving just 15 percent or so of flat plains for farming and development. The Han River is perhaps the most important in South Korea, since it flows through Seoul and provides water for some 15 million Koreans. By contrast, the most important river in North Korea, the Amrok, forms much of the border with China: Smugglers often cross the frozen river in winter to move people, products, and money into or out of North Korea.

Introduction 11

In contrast to the political system of North Korea, the one in South Korea features openness and freedoms, and all citizens have the right to choose government leaders, political ideologies, and religions. Indeed, South Korea has grown into a model of democratic stability and political action due to its citizens' unhappiness with government corruption. South Korea has rapidly evolved into a modern, ultra-high-tech nation. Its scientists help to produce new cars, electronics, medicines, and computers. Few nations are more plugged-in than South Korea, since its Internet service is the fastest in the world.

Even so, life is not all happiness on the southern side of the 38th parallel. Dissatisfaction over the division between the wealthy and the poor is growing, young people struggle to find good-paying jobs, and the work-life balance is heavily tilted toward work rather than life. Fewer and fewer women are choosing to have children, leading to a demographic crisis that could drastically destabilize South Korea's progress. As South Korea changes from moment to moment, many are frustrated by the advance of modernity, and others question whether South Korea can retain its independence of culture, language, and ethnicity in the face of the pressures of the world. Many South Koreans feel outside influences should be

Not only are elections legal in South Korea, voting is encouraged.

12 *Nations in the News:* **THE KOREAS**

Citizens attach prayer ribbons to the chain-link fence near the border. The fence, covered in barbed wire, holds messages of hope, dreams, and wishes for the unification of North and South Korea.

kept to a minimum. For others, the better solution for South Korea is to export its culture just as it exports cars and televisions: The recent waves of K-pop music groups and the growth of e-sports reflect how the world is increasingly tuning in to South Korea.

Reunification of the Korean Peninsula is a dream shared by many, but not all. Neither North Korea nor South Korea is willing to be subordinate to the other's government. The Chinese do not totally trust North Korea but prefer it nevertheless to a unified, capitalist Korea. Many South Koreans question the merits of reunification if it means they would have to bear the tremendous financial burden of lifting North Korea out of its desperate poverty. Attempts by the United Nations, the World Bank, or South Korea's Ministry of Unification to pull the nations together and work out a road map for peace and unity have made little progress. Sanctions, trade embargoes, and cutting off aid have not been enough to convince North Korea to change its plans. If there are any voices of dissent within North Korea itself, they are either shut down immediately or not made known to the outside world.

The situation in Korea today remains a stalemate. North Korea controls the fourth-largest army in the world by size, believing (or at least promoting the belief) that the war may flare up again at any time. The demilitarized zone (DMZ) between North and South Korea

Introduction

is studded with bases, minefields, and monitoring technology. While North Korea's nuclear weapons are of great concern, their conventional military artillery placed behind the DMZ could easily attack a major city like Seoul. The two Koreas have skirted dangerously close to open conflict, such as in 2010 when South Korea accused North Korea of attacking a naval vessel and killing 46 sailors. The fear of aggression from North Korea has been a primary factor in Japan's initiative to amend its constitution and rebuild its military, which officially had been disbanded since the conclusion of World War II; it is not clear whether this would backfire and drive North Korea to further aggression.

The Koreas are fairly resource poor and totally lacking in oil. South Korea imports most of its energy, while North Korea relies on small coal deposits for its (meager) electrical output. The Koreas are not entirely resource poor, however, with coal, tungsten, and graphite found in large quantities. Limited energy and mineral wealth has not stopped South Korea from becoming the fourth-largest exporter of steel in the world despite producing fewer than one million tons of iron per year (by contrast, Australia produces 800 million tons of iron per year). While North Korea is estimated to be sitting on about 10 trillion dollars in mineral wealth, from coal to gold to rare earth metals, a UN ban on mining limits its ability to dig up and sell these resources—although, like many other punishments laid onto North Korea, there is no way to know how effective this ban has been.

Each Korea is a small nation with a relatively high population and limited land usage, giving it few options for land management. Due to the mountains, some two-thirds of the Korean Peninsula is not occupied by cities or farmland and instead remains forested. Almost all arable land in both countries, however, has been developed to provide food for their populations. Even so, food self-sufficiency in both nations remains low. The combination of mountainous terrain and limited farmland means that the majority of South Korea's population, about 80 percent, lives in cities. By contrast, North Korea's rural population is higher, perhaps 40 percent, with much more land devoted to agriculture.

While at least 10 South Korean cities have populations of over one million, only North Korea's capital, Pyongyang, home to Kim Jong-un and his supporters in North Korea's Communist government,

Nations in the News: THE KOREAS

The gate in Kumsusan Memorial Palace of the Sun in Pyongyang, North Korea. This is the tomb of Kim Il-sung and Kim Jong-il.

reaches this target with a population of over three million. Pyongyang features North Korea's only international airport, although it has flights traveling only to and from China. Hamhung, on the eastern coast of North Korea, is an important city for industry as well as shipping. While the city of Kaesong is not large, with just 100,000 people, it is a crucial area for history, featuring the remains of the first human inhabitants of the Korean Peninsula as well as the Manwoldae Palace, capital of the first unified kingdom, Goryeo, whose name is the origin of the current "Korea."

About half the population of South Korea can be found in the metropolitan area of Seoul, a **megalopolis** akin to Tokyo or Beijing. The capital city is home to many Korean corporations like Samsung that have grown to be among the largest in the world. The second-largest city, Busan, lies on the southeastern coast and is the most important port in a nation that relies on shipping for its lifeblood. The city of Incheon has grown from a population of just a few thousand during the late 1800s to some three million today. It was the first port in Korea opened to international trade, making it very wealthy and very large in a short period of time.

The proximity of North and South Korea, coupled with the contrasts in their cultures, governmental structures, and relationships with other countries, make the region fascinating and potentially

Introduction 15

Scenes of life in a South Korean city.

volatile. Answers for the Korean conflict are few and far between. Kim Jong-un's regime may one day fall; the North Korean people may one day demand democracy and capitalism after learning about the better living conditions in South Korea; or the nation may simply continue hiding away from the world until it becomes obsolete and collapses. Yet North Korea's history of aggression, duplicity, and paranoia makes any course of action risky. Most experts agree there are no simple solutions to the problem on the Korean Peninsula.

Text-Dependent Questions

1. How does North Korean control of information affect the country's access to the internet?

2. What economic measures have the international community taken to stop North Korea's nuclear program?

3. Why do so many South Koreans live in cities instead of rural areas?

Research Project

North Korea's nuclear program is the most important aspect of the ongoing situation between the two nations and their allies. Do research about why North Korea chose to pursue a nuclear program. What was its path to acquiring these weapons?

Nations in the News:

The Koreas in the News in the 21st Century

When to End the War? North Korea, US at Odds over Path to Peace
Reuters.com, July 25, 2018

Trump—Kim Summit: US and North Korean Leaders Hold Historic Talks
BBC.com, July 12, 2018

South Korea: Former President Park Geun-hye Sentenced to 24 Years in Jail
Guardian, April 6, 2018

New Missile Test Shows North Korea Capable of Hitting All of US Mainland
CNN.com, November 30, 2017

South Korea Spy Agency Admits Trying to Rig 2012 Presidential Election
Guardian, August 4, 2017

South Korea Prepares for "Worst Case Scenario" with North Korea
CNN.com, September 13, 2016

North and South Korea Military Talks End in Stalemate
Guardian, October 15, 2014

North Korea Threatens Pre-Emptive Nuclear Strike against US
Guardian, March 7, 2013

North Korea Carries Out Controversial Rocket Launch
CNN.com, December 12, 2012

Kim Jong-il, North Korean Dictator, Dies
New York Times, December 19, 2011

CHAPTER 1

Security Issues

Few flashpoints in the world are as volatile, unpredictable, or potentially devastating as the situation between North and South Korea. To grasp the state of the two Koreas today, it is necessary to understand a complex history that began with the end of World War II and the start of the Cold War, in which the competing forces of democracy and communism tore the Korean peninsula apart. This separation, half a century old, has never fully healed. Today, the results of the relationship of North and South Korea have drawn in many different world powers and extend far past their own borders.

Words to Understand

Containment: In U.S. foreign policy, a series of strategies to prevent the spread of Soviet influence and communism during the Cold War.

Demilitarized zone: An area where military personnel, installations, and related activities are prohibited.

Industrialized: Economic description of nations that rely primarily on manufacturing for growth and employment.

Refugee: A person or people who leave a nation to escape war, imprisonment, repression, or other political strife; nations are obliged to take in refugees regardless of their origin or cause of displacement.

18   Nations in the News:

The conflict between North and South Korea has been going on for decades. Today, the countries are still divided, with each having its own national flag.

The Koreas' Security Issues at a Glance

North Korean Military Branches	Korean People's Army (KPA), including ground, naval, and air forces
North Korean Military Service	Compulsory from age 17 for both men and women; service obligation 10 years for men, to age 23 for women
North Korean Military Spending	Approximately 22 percent of GDP
South Korean Military Branches	Republic of Korea Army, Navy (includes Marine Corps), Air Force
South Korean Military Service	18–35 years of age for compulsory military service, minimum conscript service obligation of 21 to 24 months; 18–26 years of age for voluntary military service
South Korean Military Spending	Approximately 2.7 percent of GDP

19

Conflicts

The current situation in Korea is a reflection of the Korean War of 1950 to 1953, one of the hottest conflicts of the Cold War. Since there was never a formal peace declaration, instead ending in a cease-fire, the war is technically still ongoing. This war literally and figuratively split the Korean Peninsula, creating two distinct nations: South Korea, a capitalist democracy, and North Korea, a communist dictatorship.

The origins of the Korean War predate the conflict itself by decades. The roots of both North and South Korea go back to their next-door neighbor, Japan, which embarked on a series of conquests starting in the early 1900s. Japan had rapidly **industrialized** and modernized its government and military, allowing it to conquer nearby regions such as Korea, Manchuria (northeastern China), and Southeast Asia. Imperial Japan's conquests would result in the Pacific Theater of World War II, in which Japan fought the Allied Powers—including the United States and the Soviet Union—for dominance of the region. Japan lost and was forced to give up all of its territories, including Korea.

The Allied Powers agreed to govern Japan's former empire in the aftermath of the war. The Communist Soviet Union governed the northern half of Korea while the capitalist United States governed the southern half. In time, both halves of Korea held elections. The Communist leader Kim Il-sung became ruler of North Korea, while Syngman Rhee became president of South Korea.

The Korean War

World War II ended, but distrust between Communist and non-Communist nations began immediately after. This launched the Cold War, primarily between the United States and USSR. The United States wanted to limit the spread of communism through a foreign policy known as **containment**. In contrast, Soviet leaders wanted to spread communism throughout the world. Communists led by Mao Zedong took control of China in 1949. Mao was a vocal advocate for a worldwide Communist revolution. His triumph in China was a major setback for the U.S. policy of containment.

Kim Il-sung, the Communist leader of North Korea, believed the time was ripe for an invasion of the South. With approval and

20 Nations in the News:  THE KOREAS

Kim Il-sung (left), ruler of North Korea, and Syngman Rhee (right), president of South Korea.

Mao Zedong (left) supported Kim Il-sung's decision to invade the South and provided troops to assist in the fight. At right, Chinese troops cross the Yalu River, which borders North Korea and China.

support from the Soviet Union and China, the Communist army of North Korea attacked the South in June 1950. South Korea was unprepared and did not have the military equipment to match the North. In just five days, the North had almost overwhelmed the South.

Security Issues 21

The United States believed that it had to intervene militarily to prevent a Communist takeover, a Cold War belief that it would later repeat during the Vietnam War. With dozens of allied countries from the United Nations, the United States sent hundreds of thousands of soldiers along with tanks and airplanes to fight the Communist takeover. In the first few months of the war, the superior numbers, equipment, and training of U.S. and UN forces pushed the communists back nearly to the Chinese border. At this point, China itself intervened, worried about the potential for the United States to invade it as well. China sent hundreds of thousands of its own soldiers to fight and advance the Communist cause.

The next two years of the Korean War played out as a bloody stalemate. Negotiations for an end to the war dragged on between both sides as hundreds of thousands of soldiers and civilians died in the fighting. Eventually, however, both sides agreed to a cease-fire that resulted in a partition of Korea at the 38th parallel. This partition remains in place today, with the two nations divided by a **demilitarized zone** (DMZ) covered in minefields and guarded by military bases on both sides.

Into the Twenty-First Century

The hottest part of the Korean War was over by 1953. However, not all the fighting had finished. Distrust on both sides continues to this day. The United States still keeps thousands of soldiers in South Korea to protect from future Communist attacks. North Korea actively engages in espionage, kidnapping, and sabotage throughout the South, though it is difficult to know the exact scale of its operations. Occasionally, disputes have turned into shooting conflicts. In 2010, both sides fired on each other over a border dispute at Yeonpyeong Island, resulting in several deaths, although both sides' commanders quickly deescalated the situation.

Worse still, North Korea began a nuclear weapons program in the 1990s and successfully tested a nuclear bomb in 2006. While it is tremendously difficult to get intelligence information on North Korea, the CIA estimates that North Korea has nuclear weapons and may soon have the missile technology to use them to strike faraway places. North Korea's leader, Kim Jong-un (the grandson of Kim Il-sung), has often threatened to use nuclear weapons against

Nations in the News:

Secretary of State Hillary Clinton and Defense Secretary Robert M. Gates look out over North Korea from Observation Point Ouellette in 2010.

North Korea is not shy about its nuclear weapons program. In fact, Victory Day parades have showcased its missiles. Pictured here is a missile from the 2013 Victory Day parade.

Security Issues 23

South Korea, Japan, and the United States. However, most experts agree that North Korea wants nuclear weapons for protection, not to attack other nations.

Pulling Apart, Coming Together

In recent years, diplomatic efforts by South Korea, the United States, and the world have attempted to encourage or outright force North Korea to give up its nuclear weapons. A direct meeting between President Donald Trump and Kim Jong-un, the first summit meeting between both nations' leaders in history, resulted in agreements over security, denuclearization, and troops stationed on the peninsula. However, many critics are skeptical about North Korea holding up its side of the agreements since it has violated many previous diplomatic promises, including its assurances in the 1990s that it would not pursue nuclear weapons development.

In the days following the summit between President Donald Trump and Kim Jong-un, the world's media questioned whether North Korea would keep its promise to shut down nuclear missile test sites.

While most South Koreans strongly distrust and dislike the North Korean government, the South Korean government under President Moon Jae-in has taken steps toward peace and reconciliation. A 2018 summit between North and South Korea resulted in policies allowing families to reconnect across the border, potentially demilitarizing the DMZ, and an agreement to hold regular meetings on important issues. As a symbolic gesture, South Korea hosted the 2018 Winter Olympics and invited North Korea to send athletes to the competition, where they competed under a unified flag.

North and South Korea agree to formally end war.

Athletes from North and South Korea entered the Olympic opening ceremony under a unified flag of Korea at the 2018 Olympic Games in Pyeongchang, South Korea.

Security Issues

Alliances

Both North and South Korea have powerful friends. While the USSR has collapsed, North Korea still maintains a military and political alliance with China. The Chinese do not agree with North Korea on many issues, but China would rather have North Korea as a Communist buffer state that soaks up attention and military commitments. As a result, China provides North Korea with money, food, military equipment, and oil, all of which help to prop up the Communist government and keep the military ready for action. Only on rare occasions will China join the rest of the world in applying economic sanctions to North Korea, and some intelligence officials question whether China even follows through on these promises.

By contrast, South Korea is primarily allied with the United States and Japan and relies on these two powers for protection against North Korea and China. The United States views South Korea as a crucial part of its strategy to stop North Korean aggression as well as (and arguably more importantly to U.S. interests) to keep Chinese influence from growing. U.S. military bases in South Korea are part of a large ring that includes bases in Japan and Taiwan, meant to keep China's military from expanding and affecting others.

These alliances are problematic for both sides. The United States believes that North Korea probably could not survive on its own without Chinese assistance (especially since North Korea does not have oil of its own). By contrast, North Korea believes that South Korea must give up its alliances with the United States and Japan if the nation is ever to be reunified. Talks between the United States and China on the issue of the Korean Peninsula have had few results.

Previous attempts to bring nations together (including the United States, Japan, South Korea, China, and Russia) to put pressure on North Korea to give up its nuclear program have failed. It is not clear whether pressure from outsiders will ever be enough to convince the North Korean regime to change its policies. For example, the 2018 summit between Donald Trump and Kim Jong-un featured many promises from North Koreans, including the return of the remains of soldiers who died in the fighting, but North Korea has not shown any progress on this initiative thus far. North Korean diplomats are famously blunt in negotiations, often refusing even to consider political issues that they believe to be immovable, especially their nuclear program.

Interestingly, North Korea does not have positive partnerships with other Communist nations like Vietnam and Laos. It reportedly has a good relationship with Cuba, another Communist state. However, the distance between the two countries, their relative poverty, and the open question of whether Cuba will pivot from communism after the death of Fidel Castro keep Cuba from being a true military ally.

Regional Relations

Since both North and South Korea are located on a peninsula, one might think that they are separated from their neighbors both politically *and* physically. However, the stability of the two Koreas is of great importance to many nations in eastern Asia. China views North Korea as a sort of little brother: Outwardly, they are united in the Communist cause. Even so, this marriage can be rocky. In 2017 North Korea criticized its sole ally by stating that China's "reckless remarks" on the nuclear program tested North Korean patience and could result in grave consequences. Likewise, Japan worries about North Korea's aggression, especially because North Korea (and many citizens of South Korea) still harbors an intense dislike of the Japanese for the harm they did to Korea during World War II.

Furthermore, North Korea has also had exchanges with so-called rogue nations like Iran and Libya, which also have few friends and many enemies. As an example, North Korea has traded missile technology to Iran in exchange for oil, and leadership of both nations has complimented each other, despite the fact that Iran's leaders are religious authorities, and North Korea has outlawed religious practices.

South Korea, by contrast, is seen as a better friend by most East Asian nations. Its vibrant economy and great wealth means that many countries have trade deals with South Korea. Products ranging from Hyundai cars to Samsung televisions can be found throughout the world. While South Korean industry is often seen as a source of competition by both China and Japan, South Korea's strong economy and many acts of goodwill—being the only nation in the world that has gone from a net recipient of foreign aid to a net contributor of foreign aid—have made it friendly with major economies in the broader Asia-Pacific region such as Singapore, Australia, India, and Canada. South Korea's prestige is reflected in its hosting the Olympics and World Cup, being part of major trade associations such as the G20, and providing peacekeepers for UN missions—opportunities that are not afforded to North Korea.

International Relations

The Korean conflict has become a worldwide story of relations, negotiations, and potential conflict. Many nations have participated in the elusive quest for peace. One of the most compelling international stories of the North-South divide is that of North Korean **refugees**. Each year, thousands of Koreans attempt to flee from North Korea to escape the regime's extreme brutality or simply to find a better life for themselves and their families. Most cross the border into China, where they are viewed as illegal immigrants rather than refugees. As a result, Chinese police arrest them and have them sent back to North Korea, where they face imprisonment, torture, and execution.

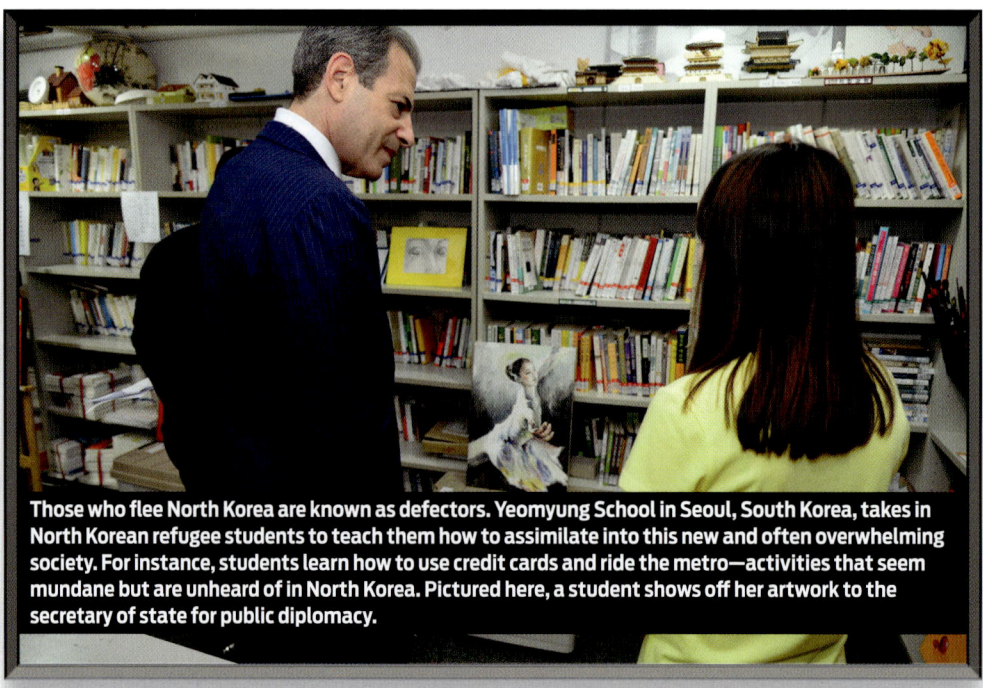

Those who flee North Korea are known as defectors. Yeomyung School in Seoul, South Korea, takes in North Korean refugee students to teach them how to assimilate into this new and often overwhelming society. For instance, students learn how to use credit cards and ride the metro—activities that seem mundane but are unheard of in North Korea. Pictured here, a student shows off her artwork to the secretary of state for public diplomacy.

Nations in the News: THE KOREAS

By contrast, all other nations in Eastern Asia have agreed that North Korean refugees should be given the freedom and the opportunity to go to South Korea to start a new life. This means that North Korean refugees need to pass through China, avoid Chinese police, and get to another nation (like Mongolia to the north or Vietnam to the south) if they wish to receive freedom. South Korea has a policy of accepting all North Korean refugees and allowing them to enter South Korean society, although adjusting to modern South Korea can be tremendously difficult for those used to living their entire lives in North Korea—some even choose to flee back across the border into North Korea!

Human Trafficking

North Korea is one of the world's worst regimes in many ways (including but not limited to repression, imprisonment, and executions), particularly on the issue of human trafficking. The North Korean government believes that all its citizens exist to serve the needs of the Communist state and the military and has no problem selling its own people for slave labor. This is done on both a large-scale level and on an individual level, and the North Korean government turns a blind eye to almost all of it.

The largest source of human trafficking is the abduction and/or sale of North Korean women to be wives or prostitutes in China. Because of the tremendous gender imbalance in China due to the favoring of male children, there are tens of millions more men than women, and competition to find girlfriends and wives is intense. Many Chinese prefer to work with North Korean traffickers to purchase a woman for a bride. Some North Korean women voluntarily go along to flee the country to find a better life, although the vast majority are tricked or kidnapped. Others are forced into sex work. Of the thousands of Koreans living in the Chinese province next to the North Korean border, an estimated 70 percent are women.

Additionally, the North Korean government sells its own prisoners to Chinese and Russian businesses looking for workers to do harsh labor. Large-scale operations such as farming, mining, and logging eagerly work with North Korean human traffickers to get tens of thousands of prisoners for grueling, dangerous, often unpaid labor. Reports from Russian logging companies suggest

Security Issues

that North Korean slave laborers receive only two days of rest per year and are punished when they cannot meet the demands of the work. Serious injuries are common and often untreated.

Finally, the North Korean government has an active strategy to disperse as many North Korean workers as possible to go abroad and earn hard cash. Since North Korea's economy is very poor, any foreign currency helps to keep its operations running. Perhaps 100,000 North Koreans (some volunteers and some forced laborers) work in this manner, returning about a billion dollars per year in foreign currency to North Korea.

South Korea also has an active human trafficking network, although it is far smaller than North Korea's. South Korean human trafficking is primarily associated with transporting Korean girls and women, within the country as well as abroad, to become sex workers. Some of these women end up in the United States. However, the South Korean government is actively pursuing human traffickers and works with the international community to put an end to both the supply and the sale of these women.

Illicit Drugs

Like many other authoritarian nations across the globe, North Korea has turned to narcotics for money. Though some North Koreans originally grew opium to be made into heroin, today manufacture of methamphetamine has become a roaring business. Since methamphetamine is not outlawed in North Korea—it is instead treated like a medicine—it is available throughout the country and has spilled over the border into China, and from there to other nations. In 2010 a North Korean plan to smuggle some 40 pounds of methamphetamine for sale in the United States was discovered. A report from 2013 suggested that North Korea's methamphetamine industry results in hundreds of millions of dollars of sales throughout the globe.

Military

North Korea's military is by far the largest in the world relative to population. All men and women must serve in the People's Army. Over one million soldiers are currently on active duty in the army, though North Korea's total population is just 25 million people.

Nations in the News:  THE KOREAS

IN THE NEWS
North Korean Diplomats and Drug Dealers

A report from 2013 laid out how North Korea specifically instructed its diplomats in foreign nations to sell drugs on the streets. Each diplomat was given around 50 pounds of narcotics and forced to earn $300,000 by selling them to demonstrate their loyalty. The government very tightly controls North Korean drug factories; the result is very high-quality narcotics that are highly sought after by drug dealers in other nations.

The Communist regime has declared that the military is its greatest priority and does not care if the rest of North Korea suffers to keep it active. The North Korean military is constantly kept on high alert, believing that a new conflict with South Korea, Japan, and the United States could break out at any moment.

By far the most dangerous part of North Korea's military is its nuclear program. North Korea is no longer a party to the Treaty on the Non-Proliferation of Nuclear Weapons, which forbids nations from developing nuclear weapons. Instead, the right to have nuclear weapons is explicitly written in North Korea's constitution. The country's road to developing nuclear weapons has become a source of national pride since crushing sanctions and lack of allies impeded its progress. It is the long-term goal of South Korea and its allies to end North Korea's nuclear weapons program, but it is not clear how this could be achieved without starting a military action that could lead to a new war. What's more, both sides have a different view of "denuclearization": South Korea, Japan, and the United States want all nuclear weapons removed from North Korea and its program shut down. North Korea sees denuclearization as only part of a much larger reward that includes withdrawal of United States forces from South Korea and a halt or even an end to the military alliance of South Korea, Japan, and the United States.

By contrast, South Korea's military is smaller but powerful and more often participates in humanitarian or disaster-relief missions than it does combat missions. South Korea keeps over half a million

Security Issues 31

At a military parade in North Korea, a portrait of Kim Il-sung can be seen in the background.

soldiers on active duty, primarily against the threat of the North. In addition, the United States maintains many military bases in South Korea to keep its commitment to the military alliance strong. South Korea has the world's 10th-largest military budget, spending about six times as much money as North Korea. The tremendous wealth imbalance of the two Koreas means that South Korea can spend far less of its total money on the military while still outspending North Korea several times over.

Terrorist Groups

The conflict in the Koreas is unique in that terrorism is rare and neither side believes it to be a viable strategy for its goals. While North and South Korea certainly have spies to carry out operations throughout each other's territories, both countries are more prepared for a military conflict than a politically motivated act of terrorism. Even so, North Korea has engaged in assassinations, including the assassination of leader Kim Jong-un's uncle, both at home and on foreign soil. North Korea has provided support and engaged in trade with other nations that directly endorse terrorism, most notably Iran; it is possible that North Korean military technology provided to Iran was later given to terrorist groups like Hezbollah. North Korea has been charged as being a state sponsor of terrorism by U.S. presidents, first by George W. Bush and then again by Donald Trump in 2017.

Text-Dependent Questions

1. Why are North Korean refugees still in danger when they escape into China?

2. Why are North Koreans so angry about South Korea's military alliance with Japan?

3. Why does South Korea spend less of its GDP on the military than North Korea, yet still has a higher military budget overall?

Research Project

Compare the human rights abuses in North Korea with another authoritarian government such as Russia, Venezuela, or Saudi Arabia. What rights are denied in North Korea but permitted in other nations? Are there any freedoms that North Koreans enjoy but other nations deny?

CHAPTER 2
Government and Politics

It is hard to imagine two governments on Earth that could be more different than North and South Korea. While South Korea is a democracy, similar to Japan, the United States, or Western European nations, North Korea is a dictatorship that does not allow its citizens any ability to control or change their government. Both governments view the other with extreme suspicion, although they have found some common ground for compromise and mutual benefits.

Government Type

A citizen of South Korea enjoys some of the greatest freedoms of any nation on Earth. By contrast, those on the opposite side of the border live under the heaviest repressions found anywhere today. How can these two neighboring nations, with a shared culture and language and history, be so different? The answer is that while South Korea has taken many steps to provide its citizens with rights, freedoms, and multiparty democracy, North Korea does not

Words to Understand

Amendment: A change to a nation's constitution or political process, sometimes major and sometimes minor.

Capital punishment: The execution of an individual for a major criminal offense, carried out by the government.

Defector: A citizen who flees his or her country, often out of fear of oppression or punishment, to start a life in another country.

34   Nations in the News: THE KOREAS

The difference in freedoms between South and North Korea is extensive. Citizens in the South have much more liberty to do what they want, including the right to protest. Pictured here, South Koreans march for peace.

The Koreas' Governments and Legal Systems at a Glance

Independence	August 15, 1945 (North and South)
National Holiday	National Liberation Day, August 15 (North and South)
National Symbol(s)	Red star of communism (North); *taegeuk* symbol (South)
Constitution	Latest adopted 1998 (North); latest approved in referendum October 28, 1987, effective February 25, 1988 (South)
Legal System	Civil law (North and South)
Voting Eligibility	Adults 17 years or older (North); adults 19 years or older (South)

believe its own citizens deserve such rights. Instead, the Communist government of North Korea believes that its people exist only to keep it in power.

South Korea's democracy is widely considered one of the most stable and least corrupt governments in the world. Like most other democracies, the country relies on a three-tier division of power and authority among the legislative, executive, and judicial branches. Power is not totally held in the hands of the central government because some authority is given to local cities and districts. Elections take place to select leaders at both the local and national levels. This development, however, has a long and slippery history, and South Korea occasionally drifted toward authoritarian rule during the second half of the twentieth century before political reform strengthened its democracy.

By contrast, North Korea's Communist dictatorship is unique among world governments for several reasons, none of which are positive. The North Korean Communist Party, like most other Communist governments, believes it has the sole authority throughout the nation and does not permit other political parties or candidates to ever gain office. Unlike most other Communist states, supreme power in North Korea is hereditary: The Kim family has ruled North Korea for

Men and women exercise their right to vote in South Korea.

Portraits of Kim Il-sung and Kim Jong-il can be seen throughout North Korea. Portraits like these are central to the *Juche* philosophy.

Learn about the ideology of Juche.

the past half-century like kings. North Korea's current dictator, Kim Jong-un, is the grandson of Communist revolutionary Kim Il-Sung, who fought against the Japanese during World War II and invaded South Korea in 1950 to establish a Communist state over all of the Korean Peninsula. Kim Jong-un controls North Korea's military, police, press, and politics, meaning there is virtually no way for North

Government and Politics

Koreans to remove him from power. The North Korean philosophy of *Juche*, which can roughly be translated to "self-reliance," teaches citizens that the government keeps them independent and safe; in turn, they must support the government all their lives.

Constitution

In 1948, the South Korean government approved its constitution that calls for a parliamentary legislative body and a president as the chief executive. This constitution is amendable and was last amended in 1987, when a wave of pro-democracy protests forced the prior military regime to open up its government and allow elections; in total, there have been 10 **amendments** to the constitution to date. The Korean constitution is roughly similar to the American constitution in that it has 10 articles laying out the basic rights of its citizens, such as the right to vote, the freedom of religion, and the inability of the government to punish citizens without due cause.

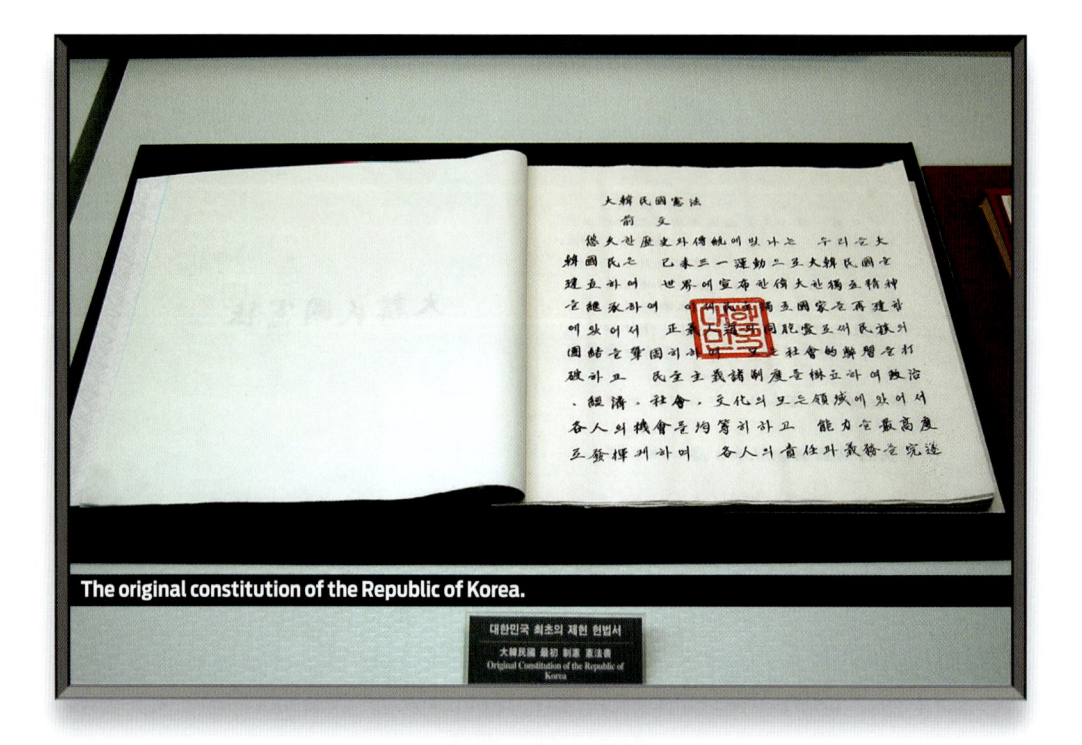

The original constitution of the Republic of Korea.

It may seem surprising that North Korea's dictatorship has a constitution, yet its national framework (named the Socialist Constitution of the Democratic People's Republic of Korea) lays out the laws of the nation and the duties of the citizenry. North Korea's constitution explicitly states the idea that it is a socialist nation, that the Communist Party of North Korea will have supreme authority to carry out all activities and directives, that all means of production are owned by the state, and that the citizens of North Korea are responsible for maintaining the standards of socialism. While North Korea's constitution guarantees freedom of expression, the right to a fair trial, and the right to elect government officials, these rights are rarely provided to citizens. It is not uncommon for North Koreans to be punished, imprisoned, and even executed for criticizing the Communist leadership of Kim Jong-un.

Additionally, North Korea maintains a political philosophy known as the Ten Principles that is arguably considered more important than its own constitution, although the two are closely interlinked. These principles put the burden on all North Korean citizens to meet its demands: to devote themselves totally to strengthening communism, to keep the authority of the supreme leader Kim Jong-un absolute and unquestioned, to obey any commands or directives, and to actively seek out threats to the party and the nation.

Independence and National Holidays

Both North and South Korea celebrate the same independence or Liberation Day, named *Gwangbokjeol* (meaning "the day that light returned"), on August 15th. It is the only holiday shared by both North and South Korea, commemorating the liberation of Korea from the Japanese Empire at the conclusion of World War II. Both North and South Korea share the harsh memory of oppression from imperial Japan, which was one of the strongest military powers in the world and used Korea for raw resources, slave labor, and sex workers (this memory is a major reason why North Korea is strongly against South Korea's military alliance with modern-day Japan). Korean Liberation Day celebrates the country's liberation at the hands of American and Soviet soldiers who defeated the Japanese.

In North Korea, it is common to have weddings on Liberation Day, as well as celebrations at both the local and national level. In South Korea, celebrations are also common, and many houses and buildings display the South Korean flag. Many museums in South Korea allow entrance free of charge, and some public transportation is also free. Both North and South Korea remember freedom fighters who died in the attempt to gain independence from Japan.

Legal System

For much of Korean history, disputes were settled at a local level with few organized laws and few hierarchies of authority. Today, South Korea has a complex civil law code based on the principles of its constitution, where all citizens are presumed innocent and must be proven guilty. North Korean law, by contrast, is tightly connected to authority within the Communist Party itself, and North Koreans are not guaranteed any legal safeguards if they break the law, including the right to be presumed innocent of a crime.

In the south, Liberation Day celebrations are lively with citizens displaying their nation's flag.

Nations in the News: **THE KOREAS**

In the North, many couples choose to get married on Liberation Day.

South Korean criminal law features several levels of courts, each with its own judicial oversight, and a Supreme Court where 14 judges interpret laws and political initiatives. At the lowest level, by contrast, municipal courts hear cases that may be relatively unimportant, with maximum punishments of 30 days in jail or a fine. South Korean criminal prosecutors are unusual in that they are part of a criminal investigation as well as a court case. This means they work much more closely with police than other nations' lawyers and have a much higher successful prosecution rate (although not as high as next-door Japan, which successfully prosecutes 99 percent of all criminal cases). **Capital punishment** is legal in South Korea, although very rare, and is carried out by hanging.

North Korean criminal law is among the most repressive in the entire world. In principle, all North Korean citizens are afforded the right to a fair trial. In reality, however, criminal punishment is meted out on the mere suspicion of having committed a crime or even simply being related to someone who has committed a crime. Capital punishment is not only permitted but very common: A huge number of offenses in North Korea can result in the death penalty, from murder to speaking out against the Communist government to watching news stories from outside the country.

Otto Warmbier, an American college student, was arrested in North Korea for attempted theft. In 2016, he was sentenced to 15 years of imprisonment with hard labor. The exact cause is unclear, but Warmbier fell into a coma while in custody. A year later, he was returned to his family and soon died from his injuries. Memorials were set up in front of his parents' home in Wyoming, Ohio.

Nations in the News: THE KOREAS

Oftentimes executions are carried out in public as a way of terrifying the population into submission and order. Imprisonment can be arbitrary and subject to the whims of Communist officials: North Korean prisons are perhaps the worst in the entire world, and it is common for prisoners to be worked, starved, and/or beaten to death. North Korean law is written to encourage all citizens to act as monitors and spies: Those who fail to report crimes can be punished just as severely as those who carry them out.

Political Parties

South Korea is typical of many other modern democracies in that it has two major political parties that compete for most national and local offices: the left-leaning Democratic Party of Korea and the right-leaning Liberty Korea Party. They combine for about 250 of the 300 seats in the National Assembly. Many third parties also hold seats and push for legislation, such as the centrist Bareunmirae Party, the reformist Justice Party, and the left-wing Minjung Party. South Korea has had several political parties in its history that are strongly communist and/or pro–North Korea, but they are not very popular and rarely receive enough votes to make an impact in creating legislation. The country has also banned some political parties believed to be directly controlled by Pyongyang with the intention of reunifying the two Koreas on the terms of North Korea.

There is only one political party in North Korea, the Democratic Front for the Reunification of the Fatherland (DFRF), which is directly controlled by the North Korean Communist government. Only members of this party are allowed to participate in elections, which are almost universally one-candidate elections in which the people's vote does not matter. North Korean **defectors** have explained that it actually is possible to vote against the ruling party in elections: Citizens must take their ballot to a special booth where they can clearly be seen and cross out the name of the DFRF candidate. However, this is such a tremendously dangerous action, with near certainty of imprisonment and execution, that no one dares to do so. The Communist government does allow some different sub-parties of the DRFR to appear on election ballots, but all these sub-parties have similar ideologies, and none advocate any changes that are not expressly endorsed by the Communist leadership itself.

IN THE NEWS
North Korean Elections

Even if they are fraudulent, North Korea does have elections. Many North Koreans participate in the elections to determine members of the national parliament, who agree to carry out directives from Communist and military leaders. These North Korean voters have no idea how free and fair elections work in other nations and proudly believe they are doing their civic duty.

Executive Branch

Like many contemporary democracies, South Korea has given its president a wide variety of executive powers, most related to national defense, balanced by checks on his or her authority. Each president in South Korea is directly elected by the people to a five-year term, after which he or she is not eligible for further re-election. Further executive power is given to the prime minister, who is appointed

Former President Park Geun-hye was forced to resign after her involvement with bribery and corruption.

Nations in the News: **THE KOREAS**

The people of South Korea took to the streets to protest President Park Geun-hye (top and bottom).

Government and Politics 45

Current President Moon Jae-in during his presidential campaign.

by the president and serves a role roughly similar to that of a vice president. The South Korean president is the commander in chief of the military and the sole member of the South Korean government with the authority to declare war. Interestingly, the president is also given the responsibility of working toward the reunification of the nation. The current president is Moon Jae-in. South Korea is one of only a few nations in the world that has elected a female head of state: Park Geun-hye won the 2013 election for the presidency, although she proved tremendously unpopular and was eventually forced to resign. She was later imprisoned on account of bribery and corruption.

In North Korea, the head of state is the reigning member of the Kim dynasty, Kim Jong-un. He has a number of official titles, including supreme leader, that all relate to his power and authority. Kim Jong-un is also chairman of the Worker's Party of Korea, meaning he is the head of both the nation and the national Communist Party, and chair of the Central Military Commission, meaning that he controls

Nations in the News: **THE KOREAS**

the North Korean military. There are virtually no checks on his power as head of state: The national constitution explicitly states that all North Koreans must work on his behalf to increase his power, to build up both the state and the army, and to follow his commands.

Legislative Branch

South Korea's National Assembly serves as the government body for creating laws. Every four years, South Korean voters elect 300 assemblymen and -women to serve as representatives for their districts and their political ideologies. Candidates for the Assembly must be at least 30 years old. Previously, during South Korea's military regimes of the twentieth century, the assembly could be dissolved by the president, effectively giving sole power to the executive branch. Today, the assembly cannot be dissolved and has a much greater role in South Korea's robust democracy. Members present bills to the speaker of the assembly, where they are debated and amended before being passed into law or rejected. Like most other democracies, South Korean political parties must forge legislative alliances, both within their party and with other parties, to get their desired laws passed.

North Korea's Supreme People's Assembly functions, in theory, on the same legislative footing as its southern counterpart. In reality, the Communist leadership holds power and sets forth its legislation. This legislation is passed by the Supreme People's Assembly with effectively no debate or changes. As such, the North Korean Assembly is seen as a "rubber stamp" that exists only to make Kim Jong-un's policies official (the same is true of Communist China's National People's Congress, which votes to make official the decisions of the topmost members of the ruling Communist Party). Members are elected by the population and serve five-year terms. Unlike South Korea's Assembly, which is in session for most of the year, the Supreme People's Assembly meets just once or twice a year, and only for a few days, since its role in the government is minor and superficial.

Judicial Branch

South Korea's independent judiciary is one of the national government bodies that acts as a check and balance on the other two. The Supreme Court has a chief justice and 13 associate justices

Government and Politics

The emblem of the Korean Supreme Court.

who rule on the most important national issues and act as the court of final appeal, while its Constitutional Court deals directly with issues concerning the South Korean constitution and determines issues involving impeachment of government officials. All justices, including the chief justice, are nominated by the president and must be approved by the National Assembly. Unlike Supreme Court justices in the United States, who serve for life, South Korea's Supreme Court justices serve for just six years, although their term can be renewed (although the chief justice position can be held only once and not renewed).

Nations in the News: **THE KOREAS**

North Korea's judicial branch is based on the legal model established by the Soviet Union. North Korea's Supreme Court is not independent of Communist leadership but has far more authority than the rubber-stamp assembly (although the assembly selects members of the Supreme Court). North Korea's Supreme Court is tasked with supervising the lower courts throughout the country, although it does not have the power to either interpret law or declare actions of the government illegal. All trials involving foreigners are held before North Korea's Supreme Court. Given the murkiness of North Korea's government, foreign officials are still not entirely clear how many justices serve in the Supreme Court, although it has been determined that there is a chief justice and that all justices serve a term of five years. Whenever a citizen is charged with a crime against the state, the Supreme Court will be the only appeal court (although many North Korean citizens are not given the right to appeal their case).

Text-Dependent Questions

1. Can North Koreans vote against the Democratic Front for the Reunification of the Fatherland?

2. What rights are promised to North Korean citizens in their national constitution?

3. What is the only holiday shared between North and South Korea?

Research Project

Look up some of the principles of the North Korean *Juche* ideology. Explain how this ideology is taught to North Koreans. How does it help to keep the North Korean government in power?

Government and Politics

CHAPTER 3
Economy

Like many other divides on the Korean Peninsula, South and North Korea could hardly be less similar in terms of their economies. South Korea is one of the wealthiest nations in the world, where major corporations like Hyundai and Samsung export their products around the globe, and has the fourth-largest economy in all of Asia. It is often favorably compared with next-door Japan, another economic power, due to the similarity between their economic structures. North Korea is one of the poorest nations in the world (depending on the metrics used, perhaps the poorest overall), and the majority of its population live in poverty on a level akin to residents of failing nations in sub-Saharan Africa or Central America. The average South Korean earns as much as 50 times

Words to Understand

Commodities: Raw products of agriculture or mining, such as corn or precious metals, that can be sold on the market.

Famine: Period of extreme lack of food, putting populations at risk of starvation.

Propagandist: A person who disseminates government-created communications, like TV shows and posters, that seek to directly influence and control a national audience to serve the needs of the government, sometimes employing outright falsehoods.

Protectionist: Actions on behalf of a government to stem international trade in favor of helping domestic businesses and producers.

Nations in the News: THE KOREAS

The opening of the Korean Stock Exchange.

The Koreas' Economy at a Glance

Currency	North Korean won, South Korean won
Inflation Rate	n/a (North); 1.9 percent (South) (2017 estimate)
Labor Force	14 million (North) (2014 estimate); 27.75 million (South) (2017 estimate)
Overall Unemployment	25.6 percent (North) (2013 estimate); 3.7 percent (South) (2017 estimate)
Imports	Petroleum, coal, machine parts, grain (North); petroleum, semiconductors, natural gas, coal, steel, computers, wireless communication equipment, automobiles, fine chemicals, textiles (South)
Exports	Minerals, metallurgical products, textiles, agricultural and fishery products (North); semiconductors, petrochemicals, automobile parts, ships, electronics, plastics (South)
Agricultural Products	Rice, corn, potatoes, wheat, soybeans, pulses, beef, pork, eggs, fruit, nuts (North); rice, root crops, barley, vegetables, fruit, cattle, pigs, chickens, milk, eggs, fish (South)
Industries	Military products, machines, electric power, chemicals, mining, metallurgy, textiles (North); electronics, telecommunications, automobile production, chemicals, shipbuilding, steel (South)

more money than the average North Korean—but with details about North Korea's economy scarce and subject to immense speculation, it can be impossible to know the depths of its poverty for certain.

Currency and Banking System

Both North and South Korea use the same term for their money, *won*, a word that has the same root word (meaning coin) as the Chinese term *yuan* and the Japanese term *yen*. Both North and South Korea print their own banknotes from their central banks in their respective capitals of Pyongyang and Seoul. Both nations have an approximate value of about 1,000 won per U.S. dollar (although North Korea has both a face value and a black-market value for exchange), primarily due to rapid inflation.

Aside from these three details, the two nations' currency and banking have no other similarities. The South Korean won is not

These banknotes and coins are currently in circulation in South Korea.

as popular for worldwide exchange as the yuan or yen but is nevertheless eagerly accepted by investors. By contrast, it is almost impossible to get North Korean won outside of North Korea itself: It has virtually no value as a medium of exchange except for currency collectors. In fact, North Korea has explicitly made it clear that only North Koreans are to use the won. Foreigners who come to the country must use a separate foreign exchange certificate to buy goods, an echo of the policies of the Communist Bloc during the height of the Cold War.

South Korean banks are major engines of the nation's economic power. South Korea has three government-run banks along with six major private banks with nationwide service; local banks and major foreign banks can also be found throughout the country. Bank reform in the late 1990s following the Asian financial crisis has improved the health of South Korean lending, inflation, and availability of credit. Like most modernized nations, the vast majority of South Koreans rely on banks for loans, investments, savings, and access to credit.

North Korean banks, by contrast, can be counted on one hand. The Central Bank provides valuable services like issuing notes and credit cards, with several dozen branches throughout North Korea. Smaller local banks service only large cities, and many serve as fronts for smuggling and money laundering, bringing in foreign currency that can be used by North Korea's Communist leadership for major purchases.

Labor Force

South Korea is a nation with extremely low unemployment at just 3.1 percent, far lower than the global average or even the average of the Organisation for Economic Co-operation and Development (also known as OECD, a collection of the world's wealthiest nations). Many factors contribute to South Korea's low unemployment: a social belief that employment and work to support the self and the family is of paramount importance; one of the world's best education systems; and the ongoing economic growth that steadily creates new jobs across many different sectors. South Korea's labor force is not all rosy, however. It (like Japan) is plagued by the "workaholic" philosophy where employees are expected to contribute far more

Similar to American banknotes, Korean banknotes feature images of prestigious persons. This North Korean 1,000 won banknote, from 2015, featured the face of Kim Il-sung.

than the typical 40-hour workweek to their employers. South Korean workers perform some 2,000 hours of work per year, higher than any nation except Mexico, although their per-hour productivity is among the worst in the world—as is their suicide rate, due primarily to frustration and exhaustion. South Korea's government has attempted to address this issue by lowering the maximum amount of hours per workweek from 68 to 52. However, it is not clear if this will make a major difference, since many workers are expected to

Nations in the News: THE KOREAS

do extra hours of work without reporting it or receiving extra compensation. Furthermore, youth unemployment represents a growing concern, as young adults who fail to grasp a career handhold early on are at risk of being left behind.

All North Koreans are expected to work hard on behalf of the Communist government and the Supreme Leader Kim Jong-un. In some cases, this means performing slave labor for little or no wages. In other cases, it means being worked to the brink of starvation. Even so, North Korean unemployment is difficult to estimate since so few North Koreans work in the formal sector. According to formal reports from the North Korean government (which are almost certainly doctored), the unemployment rate in North Korea is about 4 percent. By contrast, the Central Intelligence Agency's reports (which also may not be wholly accurate) list the unemployment at around 25 percent. Since North Korea is a socialist economy in which the government commands the output and lays out production targets, every citizen in North Korea is theoretically capable of

North Korean laborers working on a construction site.

working to support these goals. But it is not always clear whether there is money to pay them or whether there are more lucrative options for work like black-market smuggling.

Poverty

Unlike some rich nations, South Korea does not have an advanced welfare state that minimizes the burdens of poverty. Even so, only about 15 percent of the population today is in absolute poverty, about the same as in the United States, a reflection of the strong South Korean economy and the traditional ties between family members that cushion financial difficulties. Even so, poverty among the elderly in South Korea is some of the worst in the OECD: Nearly half of all South Koreans aged 65 and above live in poverty, several times more than most other industrialized nations. This is primarily because South Korea only recently introduced a public pension scheme in the 1980s and 1990s. Like many advanced economies, wealth inequality is growing in South Korea, carrying the risk that the poor will continue to become poorer while fewer and fewer people become rich.

For all the criticism of South Korean poverty, it pales in comparison to that in North Korea. While there is no shortage to the problems affecting North Korea, poverty may be the most widespread. The majority of North Korea's citizens make so little money that the national average for wages is little more than a few dollars per day. Perhaps half the population lives below the poverty line. As a reflection of this trend, the average life expectancy in North Korea has fallen by five years since the 1980s. The Communist government does not care whether its population lives in poverty. With a major **famine** approaching, Kim Jong-un's **propagandists** have told North Koreans that they may need to eat the roots of grass to survive. The contrast of starving citizens against the billions of dollars spent on North Korea's nuclear weapons program is perhaps the most serious criticism in the international community of Kim Jong-un's dictatorship.

Agriculture

Neither North nor South Korea is a suitable region for mass agriculture. Both are mountainous with relatively poor soil. Agriculture

It's difficult to pinpoint the level of poverty in North Korea; however, a few facts pop up here and there. Here, people wash their clothing in the Yalu River.

Kimchi, a favorite food in Korea, is a fermented cabbage dish that can be found in many supermarkets.

Economy 57

Markets thrive in South Korea. Vendors sell prepared food as well as fish, fruit, and other goods.

accounts for less than 3 percent of South Korea's GDP, about half the rate of agricultural value in the United States. With so little money being made by farmers, South Korea has adopted a **protectionist** attitude about its own agriculture, which cannot easily compete on the global market, especially not with next-door China producing inexpensive foodstuffs. For example, while the fermented cabbage dish kimchi is perhaps the best-known South Korean food, most kimchi on supermarket shelves comes from China. Little of South Korea's agriculture is exported due to competition and the lack of major international markets for Korean food. About 6 percent of South Korea's population works in agriculture. The trend of agricultural workers moving into new cities and new industries for better pay and living conditions, a common trend throughout the industrial world, is ongoing in South Korea.

Geography limits North Korean agriculture and frequently leaves the nation with less food produced than its people require. Despite North Korea having only about 15 percent arable land for agriculture,

This topographic map of Korea shows how rough the terrain truly is. This terrain makes farming difficult.

Experience the North Korean Jangmadan.

it is a major occupation for North Koreans, with 25 percent of its total labor force involved. Agriculture is arguably the foundation of North Korea's weak economy, since the *Jangmadang* farmers markets allow farmers to sell their goods, both legally and illegally, and earn more money than they might be able to from other industries. Most farming is done on the western lowlands where staples like rice can be grown. Interestingly, the introduction of the potato to North Korea's farms has been tremendously successful overall, though it has not been enough to mitigate frequent shortages of food. Famine in North Korea is a frequent occurrence. Floods and crop shortages in the 1990s led to the death of millions and the attempt of countless North Koreans to flee the country in search of food.

Industries

South Korean industries, from shipbuilding to technology to automobile manufacturing, are some of the most advanced and dynamic in the entire world. Shipbuilding is one of South Korea's most dominant industries, and the small nation commands a staggering 50 percent of the global shipbuilding market. While companies like Hyundai and Samsung are better known for making cars and televisions, their shipbuilding divisions account for a major proportion of their income. Hyundai Heavy Industries is the world's largest shipbuilder by both revenue and output. South Korea was a relative newcomer to the car-manufacturing business, but the industry grew quickly. Today, South Korea is the

South Korea's Hyundai Heavy Industries' shipyard.

sixth-largest automobile manufacturer in the world, producing four million cars annually. South Korean military armaments are increasingly becoming a lucrative business, with sales partners ranging from the United States to Russia to Singapore. Despite North Korea's greater financial commitment to its military (relative to total economies), South Korea inarguably has superior military technology and exports several billion dollars' worth of military hardware per year.

North Korean industry remains relatively primitive. Like in fellow socialist nations with planned economies, its industries do not exist to pursue profits or develop new technologies but rather must serve the needs of the state. Unlike its neighbor China, which has relaxed its control of the economy and established independent areas for industry and manufacturing, North Korea has failed to adopt any major reforms that could increase output. Instead, it relies on the manufacture of both light and heavy goods, primarily to be sold to its own population, although its industries do sell goods abroad when they can find willing trade partners. North Korea's garment industry produces low-cost clothing that can easily outcompete almost any other nation due to the extreme low cost of manufacturing in North Korea, since workers can be paid almost nothing and be forced to work around the clock. North Korea's automobile industry is puny compared to South Korea's; nevertheless, it manufactures cars, buses, trucks, tractors, and even luxury vehicles for the few wealthy North Koreans in the upper echelons of the Communist Party. A major factor limiting North Korean industry is the constant shortages of energy and electricity, as the availability of fuel like oil and coal is very limited, even for major cities like Pyongyang.

Commodities

Neither North nor South Korea is especially reliant on any **commodities**. This is because the Korean Peninsula is a resource-poor region: Very little metal can be found throughout the Korean Peninsula, no significant oil deposits are nearby, and agricultural output for both nations is limited by lack of space and good soil. Both nations must buy most commodities from overseas markets. There are just a few exceptions for each nation: North Korea has fairly strong production of coal, while South Korea has a large copper market, accounting for about 5 percent of the global trade in copper. North Korea may have as much as 10 trillion dollars in mineral wealth below its surface but is officially banned from mining and selling metal due to UN restrictions, though it is almost certain that it has continued to do so in secret.

Imports and Exports

While economic success isn't measured by the number of exports relative to the number of imports, South Korea might be the most successful nation on the planet if it were. Its economy is almost totally oriented toward exporting manufactured goods and technology. As a result, South Korea boasts one of the strongest trade surpluses in the entire world, earning billions of dollars more per month in goods sold abroad than goods purchased from abroad. This does not mean South Korea does not import any goods—far from it. The small nation is poor in resources ranging from steel to oil and must import almost all raw materials it requires for manufacturing. The value added by the time South Korean companies export their finished goods is the basis of its strong economic growth. Like many other aspects of its economy, South Korea is similar to Japan in this way, since Japan also relies on importing raw materials and exporting finished products.

North Korea also suffers from a scarcity of raw resources but lacks the trading partners to perform both imports or exports. International pressure placed on North Korea due to its nuclear program and its human-rights abuses means that North Korea struggles to find nations and companies willing to do business with it. North Korea's only true trade ally is fellow Communist state China, which accounts for a staggering percentage of its trade. North Korea exports about $3 billion worth of goods to China, while in second place is India with just $70 million worth of exports. Many North Korean exports, furthermore, are illicit or outright illegal. North Korea is the only nation in the world with government manufacturing facilities for methamphetamine, while its production and sale of counterfeit U.S. $100 bills may have introduced as much as $50 million worth of counterfeit money into global circulation.

IN THE NEWS
Trade with China

North Korea is a nation without many friends. In fact, it can be argued it has a positive relationship with only one nation, China, and even that is subject to scrutiny and criticism. In 2017, trade between the two nations plummeted.

Energy

Energy is, and likely will be for the foreseeable future, a major concern for both North and South Korea. Lack of fossil fuels throughout the Korean Peninsula forces both Koreas to rely on foreign trade partners for energy. Crude petroleum accounts for a full 10 percent of South Korea's total imports, since it has almost no oil of its own, while it is the second-largest importer of liquefied natural gas in the world. This has led South Korea's government to focus and invest more thoroughly on renewable energy, which today accounts for just 3 percent of the nation's total energy production. Much of South Korea has high potential for solar energy capture due to the limited number of cloudy days throughout the winter season. Few nations rely more than South Korea on nuclear energy, which accounts for about a third of its total electricity production. South Korea is ninth in global electricity consumption.

North Korea has all the energy problems of South Korea, but they are compounded by the inability to find trade partners for fuel. North Korea relies on coal-fired plants for most of its electricity, yet shortages of both coal and electricity are common throughout the country. Interestingly, North Korea is slightly ahead of its southern counterpart in renewable energy production because of its large number of hydroelectric plants. Even so, its overall electrical production is so poor that the average South Korean consumes 10 times as much electricity as the average North Korean. This reflection is often shown by the satellite images of the Korean Peninsula, in which almost all of South Korea is lit up, while all of North Korea appears dark except for the capital city of Pyongyang, where the officials of the Communist Party (including Kim Jong-un) live.

Text-Dependent Questions

1. Why is agriculture limited in both North and South Korea?

2. What group is most at risk for poverty in South Korea?

3. Who is North Korea's most important trade partner?

Research Project

Comparisons between South Korea and Japan's economy are often made due to many similarities between industries, exports, and workers. What are key economic differences between the two nations? What industries does South Korea dominate that Japan does not, and vice versa? Research these questions, and write a brief report summarizing your findings.

Quality of Life

Quality-of-life rankings often place South Korea in favorable company with nations like Australia, Canada, or Germany. It is hard to argue, by contrast, that there are worse places to live in the world than North Korea. Like most other aspects of the two nations, the contrast between the quality of life in South Korea and North Korea is incredible—it is as if a nation as wealthy and prosperous as Norway were sharing a border with a nation as poor and restrictive as Afghanistan.

Basic Human Needs

South Korean citizens live in an industrialized democracy where the government provides many of the basics needed for everyday life, even if South Korea's **welfare state** is not as well funded as other industrialized democracies. By contrast, North Koreans may have little or no support from their government and are expected to

Words to Understand

Miscegenation: Sexual relations between people of different races.

Subsidies: Amounts of money that a government gives to a particular industry to help manage prices or promote social or economic policies.

Welfare state: A system where the government publicly funds programs to ensure the health and well-being of its citizens.

Nations in the News: **THE KOREAS**

South Koreans live 82 years on average.

The Koreas' Quality of Life at a Glance

Life Expectancy at Birth	70 years (North); 82.5 years (South)
Maternal Mortality Rate	82 deaths/100,000 live births (North); 11 deaths/100,000 live births (South Korea)
Child Mortality Rate	22 deaths/1,000 live births (North), 3 deaths/1,000 live births (South)
Mother's Average Age at First Birth	N/A (North); 31 (South)
Access to Contraception	78 percent of women aged 20–49 (North) (2014); 79.6 percent of women aged 20–49 (South) (2015)
Obesity	6.8 percent (North) (2016); 4.7 percent (South) (2016 estimate)
Poverty	N/A (North); 14.4 percent (South) (2016)
Drinking Water	Improved for 99.7 percent of population (North); improved for 97.8 percent of the population (South)
Sanitation	81 percent of population (North); 100 percent of population (South)
Electricity Access	30 percent of total population (North); 100 percent of total population (South)
Years of Education	11 (North); 17 (South)
Mobile Cellular Access	14 subscriptions per 100 inhabitants (North); 120 subscriptions per 100 inhabitants (South)
Internet Access	N/A, highly restricted (North); 89.9 percent of population (South)
Broadcast Media	State-owned with no independent media (North); multiple private and public networks (South)

work sunup to sundown on behalf of the state with a bare minimum of support. The ability of both nations to meet basic human needs can be contrasted by their life expectancies: South Korean men and women live an average of 82 years, one of the longest rates in the entire world. Across the border in North Korea, life spans are a full decade shorter.

Nutrition and Basic Medical Care

South Korean agriculture is too small and too inefficient to supply the food needs of the entire nation, providing only about a third of all food consumed in South Korea. It is unlikely that it could become self-sufficient in food production any time in the near future. South Korea imports most food from China, but also from Australia, Canada, the United States, and Thailand, giving it access to many different markets and many types of meats, grains, and produce. Importing food is not cheap: Foreigners are often amazed to walk through South Korean marketplaces and see high price tags for relatively nonexotic foods like apples and bananas. Even so, there is little fear of food insecurity throughout most (if not all) of South Korea due to its many trade connections. The average South Korean consumes 3,000 kilocalories of food per day.

Food insecurity, by contrast, all but defines North Korean life. Like South Korea, Kim Jong-un's dictatorship lacks enough arable land to produce the food needed for its entire population. Unlike South Korea, North Korea spends very little money importing food to make up the difference. As a result, the average North Korean consumes 2,000 kilocalories of food per day—two-thirds the amount of a South Korean counterpart, and almost half the amount of the average American. The great famine of the 1990s, referred to as the March of Suffering in North Korea, highlighted both the nation's food insecurity and the government's apathy about it—waiting years before appealing to the United Nations for emergency food aid following the starvation deaths of untold numbers of its population. Food aid to North Korea peaked in 2001 with about 1.5 million tons delivered. However, rampant corruption, theft, and black-market profiteering by North Korean officials resulted in cutoffs of food aid. Lack of access to food has led to many health problems, such as reduced immunity to disease and

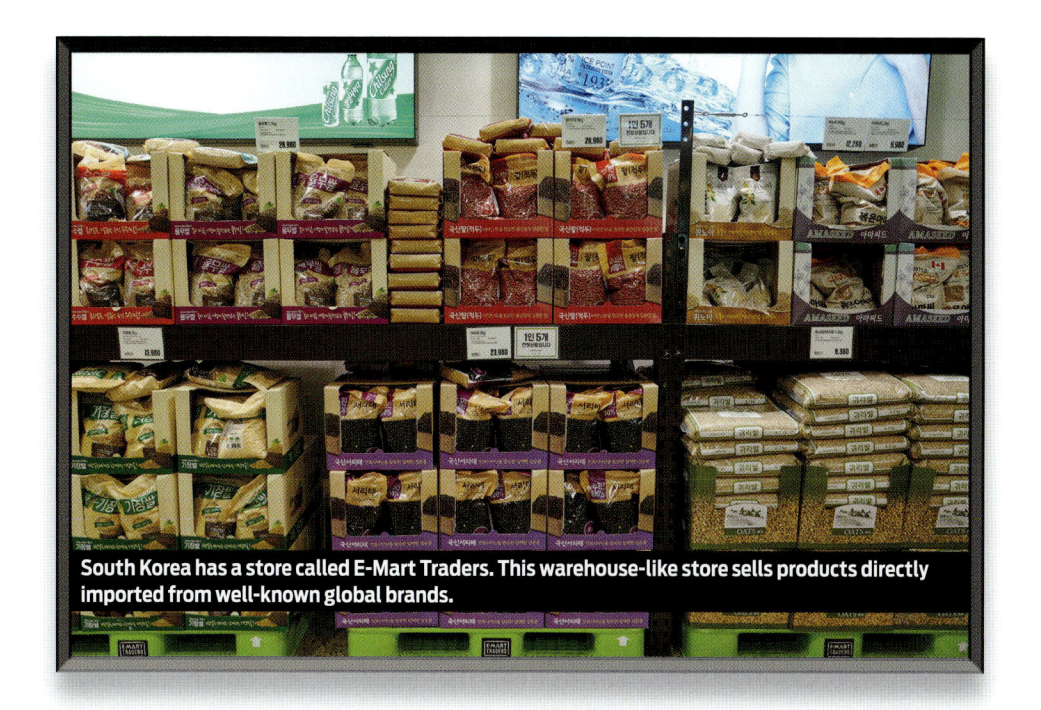

South Korea has a store called E-Mart Traders. This warehouse-like store sells products directly imported from well-known global brands.

stunting: The average North Korean is about two inches shorter than the average South Korean.

Health care in South Korea ranks among the best in the world: No nation in the OECD has better access to health care. All citizens are covered under the mandatory National Health Insurance platform, while private insurance is also available. Many major South Korean corporations have their own insurance division to cover employees and offer services to the general public. Prescription medication is relatively inexpensive in South Korea due to government **subsidies** that cover the cost of drugs. South Korea is interesting in that it is the only nation to offer universal health care with components of both Western and Eastern medicine.

While all North Korean citizens are constitutionally guaranteed health care, the overwhelming majority must pay for services they likely cannot afford. Just 3 percent of North Korea's GDP is spent on health care, compared to 7 percent in South Korea and 10 percent in Japan. While the early days of Kim Il-sung's Communist dictatorship focused on building infrastructure like hospitals and

Quality of Life 69

clinics, his grandson Kim Jong-un has not continued the trend. Most hospitals in North Korea were built 50 or more years ago, and most face chronic shortages of medicine, supplies, electricity, and even water. There are only a few success stories of North Korean medicine, such as its aggressive vaccination campaigns. Very few North Koreans die from diseases like cholera or malaria that are rampant in most underdeveloped nations. In fact, the typical North Korean causes of death read similar to those in Western nations, with cancers and cardiovascular diseases ranking at the top.

Water and Sanitation

Seasonal drought affects both North and South Korean water quantity and quality, but their proximity to monsoon rains makes it possible to make up the deficit several times over. The monsoons do not unleash the amount of water in the Koreas that they do in Southern and Southeastern Asia, but they nevertheless deliver a year's worth of rain in just three months. South Korea has successfully met its needs for drinking, cleaning, and manufacturing by becoming one of the most efficient rainwater collectors in the

About a quarter of North Koreans must still gather and carry water by hand, such as from a well.

world. Many artificial reservoirs throughout South Korea provide emergency supplies of water. There are few natural lakes and little groundwater, making it imperative to engineer water-storage sites. South Korea is also a global leader in both tidal energy harnessing and aquaculture, since it is surrounded on three sides by the ocean. Its sanitation facilities are also world class. At least 100 sanitation facilities were built between 1998 and 2008. Today, South Korea's greatest sanitation challenge is reducing its electrical and water costs, rather than expanding these services to meet any greater parts of the population.

North Korea relies more on river systems to deliver fresh water than the South. Much of North Korea's water-delivery infrastructure is degraded, damaged, or outright destroyed by years of neglect and natural disasters. Perhaps a quarter of North Koreans must rely on gathering and carrying water by hand rather than having it pumped into their homes, with much greater access to clean water in cities than in the rural population. North Korea reports that all its peoples' homes have adequate sanitation, yet reports of communal latrines and human waste entering the water table are common. Many North Koreans dig wells too close to latrines and drink contaminated water. As a result, one of the leading causes of death for children below the age of five in North Korea is diarrhea.

IN THE NEWS
South Korean Sanitation

After the end of the Korean War, South Korea did not have a single sewer line. Today, 90 percent of its waste is treated. This incredible success was attributed to Korea's investment in infrastructure, education of engineers to manage wastewater systems, and robust policies of regulation and oversight.

Shelter

Growing into a modern, wealthy nation has solved many of South Korea's problems but has created many new ones in turn. Like many similar compact nations, a major concern in South Korea is housing, where demand far outpaces supply. A full 20 percent of the nation's population lives in the capital city, Seoul, where housing prices have risen by a quarter in the past four years, and an average apartment today costs over half a million dollars. South Korea's politicians have fluctuated between trying to lower the economic burdens on existing homeowners to stimulate the economy and rapidly building new housing units to ease the squeeze. Construction investment in South Korea is growing far faster than the economy itself as the government attempts to prevent a property bubble (a rapid overgrowth and then collapse of housing prices) from forming as it did during the Asian financial crisis of the late 1990s.

Complicating factors is the culture of *Jeonse*, roughly translated as "key money," in which apartment tenants pay a massive up-front deposit to landlords—as much as 80 percent of the apartment's actual value—but then pay little or no rent itself. With the average cost of *Jeonse* running over a quarter of a million dollars, this system prevents the young and the poor from gaining access to property, even though the deposit is returned at the end of the lease (the owner invests the deposit and keeps the interest). The degree of risk in the system—to both landlord and tenant—has made *Jeonse* a huge roadblock to improving South Korean housing. While the government does little to help the homeless, there are very few homeless overall—perhaps only 10,000 in all of South Korea, less than a quarter of the number of homeless people in Los Angeles alone.

Since population growth and urbanization are not the major drivers in North Korea that they are in South Korea, there is less of a demand for new housing, especially outside the major big cities. However, this does not mean that the existing quality of housing is high. Many of North Korea's apartment buildings were designed and built by the Soviet Union decades ago, and many are derelict or badly outdated. The northernmost region of North Korea, next to the Chinese border, is in the midst of a property bubble as more and more North Koreans are eager to build and own homes next to China. This is a reflection of several factors, including the highly lucrative smuggling business and the hopes that better relations with China will improve North Koreans' quality of life.

Apartment houses in Seoul, South Korea. Demand for housing still outpaces supply despite increased investment in construction.

Take a peek inside a North Korean home.

Personal Safety

South Korea is regarded as one of the safest places in the world to live, with one of the lowest levels of violent crime anywhere on Earth. Mostly this low crime rate is a reflection of several aspects of the culture in South Korea, which encourages assimilation into the community and good standing among family and friends, has a

Quality of Life 73

very low unemployment rate, and has mandatory military training, including self-defense training. The homicide rate in South Korea is one of the lowest in the world, experiencing just a few hundred homicides per year, a figure the United States reaches in just 10 days. It is very difficult to own firearms in South Korea, with just one registered firearm per 100 people, and many police officers do not carry sidearms at all.

Many statistics about crime and safety in North Korea are highly dubious because they come from the government itself, which confidently states that the nation does not have crime. Lack of published and verifiable information leaves many questions about North Korea, although many conclusions can be drawn. A list of 12 public executions in North Korea for the crime of murder between 2004 and 2010 suggest that violent crime is present, although rare. As with many other aspects of their lives, the greatest security risk to North Koreans is not crime but the government, which can arbitrarily detain, imprison, and execute its own citizens without (or with a bare minimum of) due cause. The degree to which North Korea's government vigorously roots out dissent has raised questions of whether the government itself can be charged with committing political terrorism.

Personal Well-Being

Measuring happiness is a fickle endeavor at best, but the World Happiness Reports suggest that South Korea has a good deal of work to do, ranking just 52nd next to Jamaica and Russia (perhaps not coincidentally due to their social similarities, Japan is just a few slots higher). The mass brainwashing of North Korean citizens, along with the terror of criticizing their government, means that they would doubtless score much higher and perhaps even top the list.

Education

South Korea is a global leader in education in many metrics, some of which are favorable and some of which suggest significant flaws in its system. South Korea's literacy rate is practically 100 percent. Children receive an education starting at the age of four, and 99 percent of the population completes secondary education. Education is viewed as a cornerstone of South Korea society and a

A group of schoolchildren on a field trip at the Korean War Memorial in Seoul.

fundamental goal for all young people to attain. This, however, leads to immense pressure to succeed in school and to be accepted into a good university. The saying that "if you sleep three hours a night you may get into a leading university" reflects both the massive expectations and workloads put on the shoulders of every South Korean student. Children may study as much as 12 hours a day, completing public school each day only to come home to study with a private tutor afterward. As a result of the intense pressure, suicide is the leading cause of death of South Korean teenagers.

Education in North Korea is entirely state run, and its goal is just as much indoctrination as it is practical learning. North Korea's regime can stay in power only by convincing its citizens that they must strive to work for the government and that the authority of Kim Jong-un is never to be questioned. These lessons begin at an early age and help children understand the rules of life in North Korea. Defectors tell stories of classrooms in which students must denounce one another for even the most minor offenses so that they become used to the idea that privacy does not exist and all must work for the North Korean state.

Quality of Life

Information Access

South Korea's Internet is widely considered the world leader. Due to the compact urban population, it is far easier to build Internet-provider infrastructure than it is in the United States, which has a high rural population. As a result, South Korea has the world's fastest Internet services. With major homegrown tech corporations like Samsung, furthermore, about 80 percent of the population owns a smartphone, including three out of four South Koreans by the age of 12.

Access to any information in North Korea is tightly controlled by the government, which treats possession of foreign (including South Korean) media to be a capital crime. Sweeps of homes for contraband radios, phones, USB sticks, and DVDs are common. Even so, demand for foreign television shows, news, and technology is high in North Korea. Many risk their lives to smuggle foreign media into the country and sell it at a high price, sometimes with the officials turning a blind eye. South Korea actively makes efforts to educate the North Korean public by spreading its own news shows and papers across the border, sometimes by broadcasting radio signals and sometimes by primitive means like mass balloon lifts.

In many countries, a DVD collection like this would be the norm. In North Korea, however, it could land you in prison.

Nations in the News: **THE KOREAS**

Health and Wellness

With a high quality of health care, South Korean citizens have a life expectancy that is better than all but 10 other nations across the globe. Long life in South Korea reflects the people's healthy diets, high social engagement, and strong family ties. Even so, major issues in health can be found throughout the country, reflecting their national vices. About one in three adult men smoke, a much higher rate than most other nations; by contrast, fewer than 5 percent of adult women smoke. South Korea is the world's leading per capita consumer of hard alcohol. Long working hours and intense peer pressure likely contribute to the issue of alcoholism that affects 1.5 million South Koreans. Finally, air pollution is a serious concern.

North Koreans have less money for smoking and drinking, although this alone does not make them healthier. The cost and centralization of North Korean medicine, in addition to the everyday problems of malnutrition and sanitation, result in a much lower life expectancy. In 2010, a report suggested that North Korea had a tuberculosis epidemic, affecting 5 percent of the population. About the same percentage of the population has also tested positive for hepatitis.

Environment

Many industrialized nations have sacrificed environmental well-being in favor of growth, and South Korea is no exception. One of the greatest environmental issues affecting the nation today is air pollution, primarily from the compact cities but also from wind patterns that blow in so-called yellow dust from Chinese industrial zones. South Korea ranks 173rd out of 180 nations in terms of air quality. Environmental initiatives like reforestation have succeeded at redeveloping many natural parts of the peninsula damaged by urban expansion.

Many reports from North Korea suggest that the nation's environment is approaching a state of collapse. Intensive deforestation and hunting nearly any animal for food has taken a huge toll on North Korean biodiversity, and an estimated 10 percent of all North Korean animals are endangered. Satellite images have revealed that perhaps half of North Korea's forests have been cut down. Pollution of rivers has been reported as "severe." While there are fewer large cities in

A yellow haze of air pollution from Chinese industrial zones hangs over Seoul's skyline.

North Korea, air pollution is a problem in Pyongyang, especially since coal power plants are the primary source of electricity. To its credit, North Korea's government has signed the Paris Agreement and has begun investing in renewable energy.

Opportunity

The word "opportunity" means two different things on each side of the Korean Peninsula. For South Koreans, it may mean social transformation and growing to become part of the wealthy classes. Like many wealthy nations, however, South Korea's social mobility is stuck in neutral. While it is not impossible to go from rags to riches in South Korea, as in the case of former president Lee Myung-bak, it is not easy either. An economic study suggested that just two in 10 of South Korea's poorest workers saw any major rise in their economic status from 2013 to 2016. The same study found that fewer than a quarter of South Koreans believed they could advance to a higher social class based on their own attempts and talents.

For North Koreans, opportunity may be a foregone conclusion or an impossibility. This is largely due to the fact that social classes are frozen in place by the *songbun* ideology. *Songbun* is a system that divides North Koreans based on their ancestors'

Lee Myung-bak, former president of South Korea after his 2008 inauguration.

affiliations during the Korean War: Those families who served with or supported Kim Il-sung have the highest *songbun* and get the best jobs, housing, food, and opportunities within the Communist Party. Those who opposed Kim Il-sung have the lowest *songbun* and are highly distrusted. Many prisoners in North Korea come from the lowest *songbun* class. Those North Koreans fortunate enough to live and work in Pyongyang, where they can enjoy far greater financial opportunity, modern technology, and even limited access to the outside world, are almost entirely from the topmost *songbun* class.

Personal and Political Rights

Ranked 29th by the Cato Institute's Human Freedom Index, South Korea is a nation where citizens are free to comment on and criticize their government. Protests and demonstrations have played a major part in South Korea's political history, helping to bring about full democracy in the 1980s after years of semi-authoritarian rule. Efforts by the citizens to uncover corruption have led to the downfall of major politicians, including former president Park Geun-hye. It should be noted, however, that the government takes pains to prevent pro–North Korean activity and has been guilty of suppressing dissension under this pretense.

Virtually every metric on political rights would place North Korea dead last. Despite North Korea's constitutional guarantee of freedom of speech, North Korea is a police state in which open disagreement with Kim Jong-un's leadership or the power of the Communist Party can lead to imprisonment and execution. It is not uncommon for the families of these "political traitors" to also be arrested and subject to punishment. Even the most minor acts of political disobedience are protected against: It is illegal to throw away a picture of the supreme leader, meaning that a North Korean citizen is committing a crime simply by disposing of old newspapers.

Freedom of Choice

South Korean democracy is robust and provides its citizens with many choices for their leaders (although, like many democracies, two centrist parties win most votes and hold most power). Personal

In 2018, the city of Jeonju held its first Pride parade. People came out to support equality and diversity within the LGBTQ community.

freedoms are broadly respected throughout the country, with a variety of religions practiced and accepted. Gay rights and the LGBTQ community, however, have not made significant advances in South Korea. Same-sex marriage is not legal, and many men and women remain "in the closet" to prevent discrimination from their family, friends, or coworkers. While prostitution is theoretically illegal in South Korea, many different avenues for sex work have arisen, and half of all South Korean men report having paid for sex.

North Korean democracy is analogous to Iraqi democracy during Saddam Hussein's dictatorship, in which voters could choose either "Saddam" or "Not Saddam." Communist elections in North Korea feature just one candidate preapproved by the party. It is believed to be far too risky to attempt to vote for any other individual, although in theory North Koreans are permitted to do so. Until recently, North Koreans had no freedom of religion, as religion was viewed as a means of undermining the socialist state. Within just the past few years, however, North Korea has lifted this restriction in a new attempt to build positive relations with religious leaders, most notably the Vatican, and Pyongyang now has three Christian churches.

Tolerance and Inclusion

With many socially and politically conservative viewpoints prevailing throughout South Korea, aspects of intolerance have become entrenched in everyday life. Gender inequality in South Korea is notoriously poor, and the country ranks in the bottom third of all nations according to the World Economic Forum's Global Gender Gap Report. There is a very low ratio of women among working professionals or in management and executive positions, tertiary education, and government positions. Many South Koreans believe the man should be the breadwinner while the woman remains the housekeeper. South Korean women are increasingly refusing to adhere to these cultural norms and are marrying later and having fewer children, pushing South Korea's birthrate well below the replacement level.

The increase in immigration to South Korea from other East Asian nations has revealed a degree of racial discrimination as well, as about half of all South Koreans report not wanting to have a foreigner as a neighbor. Interestingly, many negative racial attitudes in South Korea are explicitly focused on Asians and Africans: Europeans and North or South Americans are viewed much more positively. There is no antidiscrimination law in South Korea preventing companies from refusing to hire foreigners, homosexuals, or women. Intolerance takes a different form in North Korea due to the *songbun* political caste system, where those with the highest status receive the most opportunity.

Mild racism in South Korea is contrasted by severe racism in North Korea, since part of the *Juche* ideology of North Korea emphasizes the importance of racial purity. North Korean women who flee the country and then are captured and returned while pregnant with a child from a non-Korean father often are subject to forced abortions due to the government's fear of **miscegenation**. It is not possible for anyone to earn citizenship in North Korea if they are not Korean themselves and were not born in North Korea.

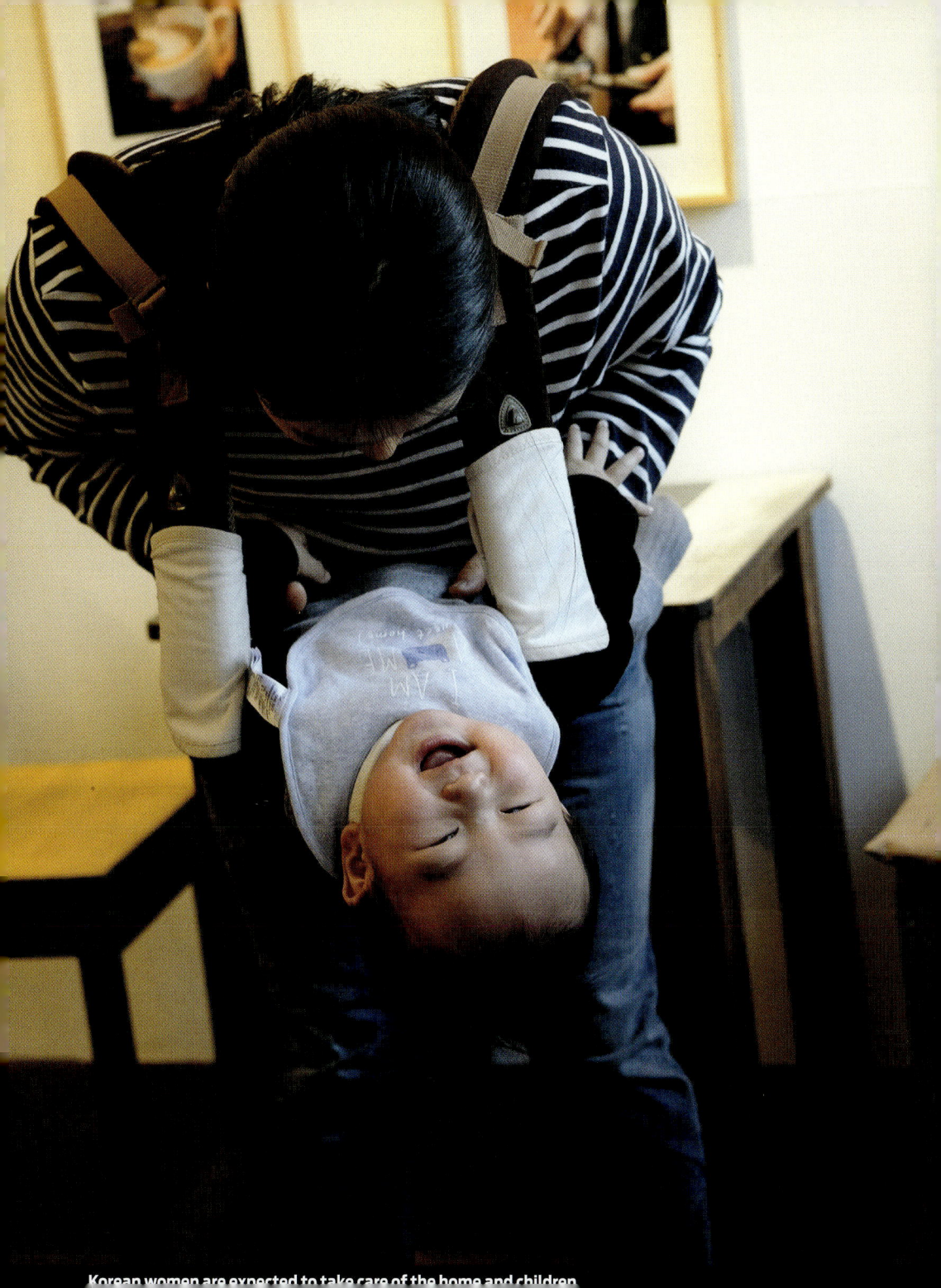

Korean women are expected to take care of the home and children

Higher Education

South Korean universities are both prestigious and competitive. About two-thirds of all South Koreans complete university, although discrimination over lower-tier schools is common. Strict entrance requirements and a comprehensive examination necessitate years of studying and are a major source of stress for South Korean teenagers. An institute's reputation and its alumni network may be the difference between a student landing an excellent job or settling for an entry-level position upon graduation.

By contrast, North Korea has very few options for higher education, and they are closed off to all but the most elite members of the Communist Party and their families. Kim Il-sung University in Pyongyang is the only institution that offers advanced master's and doctoral degrees. Despite the lack of a broader higher education system, North Korea's "homemade" technologies, including missile systems and nuclear weapons, reflect the intellectual rigor and capabilities of its scientists.

Kyung Hee University in South Korea.

Nations in the News: **THE KOREAS**

Text-Dependent Questions

1. Why does South Korea have better Internet connections than the United States?

2. What is "yellow dust"?

3. Why is it illegal to throw away a newspaper in North Korea?

Research Project

Life in North Korea depends on your *songbun*. But what exactly is *songbun*? Create a visual chart that lists out the various attributes and levels of *songbun*, indicating the type of life that a person could expect to live at each. Write an accompanying report that answers the question: How is *songbun* different from or similar to the ways your society measures social standing?

CHAPTER 5
Society and Culture

Thousands of years of shared culture compete against two very different political structures to reflect the similarities and differences between North and South Korean society. To an outsider, it may seem as if every similarity shared by the two nations is compounded by a major difference.

Birth and Death Rates

South Korea's advanced health-care system has resulted in one of the longest average life spans in the world. With a death rate of 5.5 people per 1,000, South Korea is affected by many contemporary health-care issues (including heart disease, diabetes, cancer, and respiratory diseases) but remains one of the healthiest societies in the world. However, its **birth rate** is in free fall and has raised the question of whether South Korea is in a demographic crisis. In 1960, the average Korean woman had six children; in 2018 the

Words to Understand

Asylum: Political protection for a group of persons, often refugees, that allows them to enter a country and find a new home.

Birth rate: The number of births per 1,000 members of the population.

Diaspora: The members of a community that spread out into the wider world, sometimes assimilating to new cultures and sometimes retaining most or all of their original culture.

Nations in the News: THE KOREAS

A North Korean family on International Worker's Day.

The Koreas' Society and Culture at a Glance

Population	25,248,140 million (North) (July 2017 estimate); 51,181,299 million (South) (July 2017 estimate)
Sex Ratio	94 males/female (North); 1 male/female (South)
Age Distribution	20.78 percent age 0–14; 15.59 percent age 15–24; 44.28 percent age 25–54; 9.77 percent age 55–64; 9.56 percent age 65 and over (North)—13.21 percent age 0–14; 12.66 percent age 15–24; 45.52 percent age 25–54; 14.49 percent age 55–64; 14.12 percent age 65 and over (South)
Ethnic Groups	Homogenous, with a small Chinese community and a few ethnic Japanese (North); homogenous (South)
Religions	Traditionally Buddhist and Confucian, though autonomous religious groups are almost nonexistent in favor of government-sponsored religious programs (North); Buddhist, Catholic, Protestant, traditional Korean religion (South)
Languages	Korean (North); Korean and English (South)

figure is just 1.2 children per woman, far below the replacement rate needed to keep population levels steady, let alone growing. Women have increasingly refused to accept the social norms for motherhood: a father who works almost constantly, grandparents who claim the privilege of being able to order parents around, and difficulty finding affordable daycare facilities. The average age for both marriage and motherhood has steadily been rising.

South Korea's sliding birth rates closely resemble those of Japan. Indeed, these two nations share a great deal of similarities, both social and economic, and both will grow increasingly older in the near future due to nose-diving birth rates. This will potentially create a disastrous situation where there are too many elderly people taking up too many social services and not enough young people to provide assistance and taxpayer dollars to support them. The easiest solution—increasing immigration thresholds—is extremely unpopular among both South Koreans and Japanese, both of which have explicit biases toward a racially and culturally homogenous society. South Korea accepts just 17,000 immigrants per year (Japan accepts even fewer), many of whom are married to South Korean

Korean elders take part in dance activities in a park.

Nations in the News: **THE KOREAS**

Although South Korea's birth rate is low, when women do give birth, they receive excellent health care at high-end hospitals.

nationals. Government policies in both nations to increase birth rates have seen limited success and fail to address crucial issues like the expectation that women will shoulder all child-raising duties, in addition to taking care of the house and any elderly relatives.

North Korea's birth rate is not nearly as troublesome. With an average of nearly two children per woman, North Korea's population is not at risk of rapid aging and more closely resembles the worldwide average of developed nations. North Korea's population doubled between 1960 and 1980, but famine, disease, and economic hardships have kept total population growth at just five million persons in the past 30 years. With a death rate that is about twice the average of South Korea's, however, the gulf between health and wellness in the two nations is quite stark.

Population by Age

It is a rare nation that has more elderly people than young people. South Korea has one of the widest splits found on the globe: There are more persons over the age of 65 than there are people under the age of 14. By contrast, there are about 10 million more children in

The leaders of North Korea have always been notorious tobacco smokers. Kim Il-sung was depicted holding a cigarette in this portrait.

the United States than there are seniors. The bulk of South Korea's population is working age, 25 to 54, comprising 45 percent of the total population. Low birth rates reflect economic anxiety and dissatisfaction with traditional gender roles and the family structure in Korean culture. The average South Korean woman has her first child at the age of 31, the oldest average rate of any nation in the world. For the first time in history, South Korea had more deaths in a single month than births in December of 2017. If this trend continues, South Korea's population will drop by a quarter in the next 100 years.

North Korean demographics resemble a middle-economic power (they align fairly closely to Chile's) in that the bulk of its population is young, with 80 percent under the age of 55 and 90 percent under the age of 65. Many factors contribute to North Korea's low life expectancy; separate from major issues like nutrition and access to medicine, a contributing health issue in North Korea is smoking. The majority of men in North Korea, a full 54 percent, smoke regularly (a small percentage of women do—it is seen as a cultural taboo for North Korean women to smoke). What's more, Kim Jong-un is noted as a major tobacco addict who openly chain-smokes and is often seen in public or in the newspapers with a cigarette in hand.

Nations in the News: **THE KOREAS**

IN THE NEWS
Smoking in North Korea

Most North Korean men smoke, especially Kim Jong-un; North Korea is one of the few places in the world where people can smoke almost anywhere at any time. Yet the North Korean government realizes the health dangers of this habit and is slowly trying to get its population to give up smoking

Religions

Religion in South Korea encompasses a broad diversity of beliefs with no government limitation on worship or organization. Three of the world's most popular religions can be found here in peace with one another: Buddhism, Confucianism, and Christianity. About half the Korean population reports that they follow a religion, and the government counts over 500 different faiths and sects. Buddhism first arrived in Korea in 372. Just as it did in China and Japan, it quickly proved a popular religion. Today there are thousands of Buddhist

Korean university students attend a Jeonju Confucian school.

Society and Culture

A woman prays in a Buddhist temple.

temples across South Korea. Confucianism was adopted by the Joseon Dynasty from about 1400 to 1900. Christianity arrived in Korea in the 1800s and became popular among the poorest classes; efforts by the ruling Koreans to wipe out this new foreign religion failed, and Korea today has produced the fourth-highest number of Catholic saints of any nation. Korean shamanism, or *shindo*, represents a type of folk religion where shamans act as intermediaries between the supreme god, Haneullim, and common people.

Like so many other cultural divides, the picture of religion in North Korea could hardly be a greater contrast. Religion was outlawed for most of North Korean history, ostensibly due to the dogmatic Marxist belief but truly because the ruling Kim clan and their Communist supporters fear any other authority that may interfere with their power. Today, some Buddhist, Christian, and *shindo* ceremonies are permitted. Indeed, the promotion and adoration of the Kim family is itself a religious rite in North Korea: Citizens are told that the Kims are all-powerful and all-capable; that they are perfect and continually do great things; and that all North Koreans must praise them and work on their behalf.

If the cult of Kim is considered a religion, it is the ninth-largest in the world, ahead of Sikhism. Failure to give its people freedom of religion is one of the most common criticisms of the totalitarian North Korean government. Many Christian churches in South Korea attempt nevertheless to smuggle religious material across the border in the hopes of continuing their ministry to the few Christians who worship in secret. Many of these churches also act as leaders for the intake of North Korean refugees.

Watch a traditional Korean religious ritual.

Society and Culture

Statues of the Kim family can be found across North Korea.

Ethnic Groups

Few places on Earth have less ethnic diversity than the two Koreas. Both are very homogeneous societies: Over 96 percent of the population is Korean, and only in 2007 did the total number of all ethnic non-Koreans surpass the 1 million mark. Today it is about twice that figure, with Chinese, Vietnamese, Thais, and Americans accounting for the bulk of foreigners living in South Korea. Even so, immigration to South Korea is tremendously difficult, especially for non-Asians. A North American wishing to immigrate to South Korea will find it challenging: A comprehensive language test is required, as is proof of employment, for those who wish to come to the country after marrying a Korean spouse.

 Racism among the majority ethnic groups is a familiar tale throughout much of East Asia, and South Korea is no exception. The term *danil minjok* was taught to schoolchildren at an early age and roughly translates to "one people" or "single bloodline." While this concept was used to foster national unity in eras past, it is now applied as a shield against outsiders. South Koreans are famously unwelcoming of refugees: A group of about 500 Yemeni refugees arrived on the South Korean island of Jeju in 2018 seeking **asylum**. Protests throughout South Korea revealed the intense dislike of refugees, while a petition to the president to turn away the asylum-seekers collected over half a million signatures. South Korea has accepted fewer than 3 percent of all asylum-seekers (not counting North Korean refugees) in the past 20 years.

Racism in North Korea, by contrast, is not only overt but also state-sponsored. It is part of the all-important *Juche* philosophy of self-reliance: The only path to North Korean citizenship is to be an ethnic Korean born in North Korea. There are small populations of Chinese ethnic groups, especially closer to the border, though most of these populations are dropping, emigrating to China when possible as growing economic opportunity in China is contrasted by increasing authoritarianism in North Korea. There are also small populations of Japanese: survivors of World War II and their families, Communist defectors, and the dozens, or perhaps hundreds, of Japanese nationals who have been kidnapped and sent to North Korea to teach the language and culture. Small pockets of American families, from soldiers who either deserted or were captured, can be found: Charles Robert Jenkins either deserted his post at the DMZ or was abducted in 1965, and in either event crossed into North Korea and was not returned until 2004.

Languages

Korean is the primary language of both North and South Korea. Due to the ethnic homogeneity of the Korean Peninsula, the vast majority of the population speaks Korean as a first language. South Korean schoolchildren are educated in English from an early age: American tourists are surprised to find that many young South Koreans are not only able to communicate in English but are eager for the chance to practice. The next most spoken language, Chinese, is useful in both North and South Korea due to the tremendous economic power of their neighbor, as well as the high number of Chinese visitors and permanent residents in both nations. Some older Koreans can still speak Japanese, a legacy of the colonial era, while southern cities like Busan, nearer to Japan itself, also have higher rates of bilingualism.

The dialects of Korean change throughout both North and South Korea. There are eight main dialects, analogous to the eight provinces of the Korean Peninsula: the Jeju dialect is sometimes considered so different as to be its own language. Both North and South Korean "standard" dialects correspond to their largest and most important cities, Pyongyang Korean in the North and Seoul Korean in the South. Interestingly, the split between North and South Korean has resulted in major vernacular differences, although both sides understand each other in standard conversation. The common name "Lee" in South Korea is pronounced "Ri" in North Korea. Words formed by two or more independent concepts are not separated in North Korean dialect, while they are in South Korean dialect, making the North Korean language roughly analogous to German or Swedish (relative to English) in its creation of long words.

Foods

A shortage of farming space, a lack of agricultural exports, and a smaller **diaspora** has resulted in Korean food being much less well-known than Chinese or Japanese cuisine. Without a doubt the most famous Korean food is the fermented cabbage, kimchi, which has such a great deal of flavors and seasonings that there are over 100 varieties. Like other East Asian nations, rice is a staple of practically every Korean meal, although the arid climate and mountainous terrain make it more difficult to grow than in other regions. The Korean Peninsula is surrounded by water and fishing, so seafood makes up a major part of the diets of both nations: *Jeotgal* is a common salted dish of fish, shrimp, roe, or other seafood, creating a wide variety of flavors and textures.

Food scarcity remains a fact of life in North Korea outside of major cities. Many experiments to improve the availability of food, including a bizarre attempt by Kim Jong-il in the 1990s to breed giant rabbits, have not provided long-term food security. While there are many restaurants in Pyongyang, virtually all are too expensive for the average North Korean and are instead patronized by the wealthy elite and foreign visitors. North Korea's first pizzeria opened in 2009.

Jeotgal is a popular salted seafood dish.

National Holidays

Both nations have several other national holidays in addition to Liberation Day: North Korea celebrates the birthday of Kim Il-sung, its founding father, and gives out candy to schoolchildren to mark the event. (This may be the only time all year that some North Korean children get any sweets.) They call this the "Day of the Sun," and it is a major celebration as well as a means of indoctrinating North Koreans to adhere to the *Juche* philosophy. Other holidays include the solstice, the founding of the Communist Party, and International Worker's Day. Interestingly, North Korea has shown a trend of carrying out nuclear tests on its own national holidays.

South Korea also celebrates many traditional holidays based on the solstice and the seasons, as well as New Year's, Constitution Day, and Memorial Day. South Korea also celebrates Christmas: While Christianity is fairly popular in South Korea, the religion has only a minor foothold in North Korea, since the communists believe that it undermines their authority and legitimacy.

Society and Culture

Day of the Sun celebrations in North Korea (top and bottom).

98   *Nations in the News:* **THE KOREAS**

Text-Dependent Questions

1. How is racism overt in both Koreas?
2. What is kimchi?
3. What is the second-most-common ethnic group in Korea?

Research Project

Research the *shindo* religion that is native to Korea. What are some of the elements of *shindo* belief? How is this religion organized? How do Koreans adhere to its principles and morals? Write a brief report summarizing your findings.

Series Glossary of Key Terms

Absolute monarchy: A form of government led by a single individual, usually called a king or a queen, who has control over all aspects of government and whose authority cannot be challenged.

Amendment: A change to a nation's constitution or political process, sometimes major and sometimes minor.

Arable: Describing land that is capable of being used for agriculture.

Asylum: When a nation grants protection to a refugee or immigrant who has been persecuted in his or her own country.

Austerity: Governmental policies that include spending cuts, tax increases, or a combination of the two, with the aim of reducing budget deficits.

Authoritarianism: Governmental structure in which all citizens must follow the commands of the reigning authority, with few or no rights of their own.

Autocracy: Ruling regime in which the leader has absolute power.

Bicameral: A legislative body structured into two branches or chambers.

Bilateral: Something that involves two nations or parties.

Bloc: A group of countries or parties with similar aims and purposes.

Cash crop: Agriculture meant to be sold directly for profit rather than consumed.

Central bank: A government-authorized bank whose purpose is to provide money to retail, commercial, investment, and other banks.

Cleric: A general term for a religious leader such as a priest or imam.

Coalition force: A force made up of military elements from nations that have created a temporary alliance for a specific purpose.

Colonization: The process of occupying land and controlling a native population.

Commodities: Raw products of agriculture or mining, such as corn or precious metals, that can be bought and sold on the market.

Communism: An economic and political system where all property is held in common; a form of government in which a one-party state controls the means of production and distribution of resources.

Conscription: Compulsory enlistment into state service, usually the military.

Constituency: A body of voters in a specific area who elect a representative to a legislative body.

Constitution: A written document or unwritten set of traditions that outline the powers, responsibilities, and limitations of a government.

Coup: A quick change in government leadership without a legal basis, most often by violent means.

De-escalation: Reduction or elimination of armed hostilities in a war zone, often directed by a cease-fire or truce.

Defector: A citizen who flees his or her country, often out of fear of oppression or punishment, to start a life in another country.

Demilitarized zone: An area where military personnel, installations, and related activities are prohibited.

Depose: The act of removing a head of government through force, intimidation, and/or manipulation.

Détente: An easing of hostility or strained relations, particularly between countries.

Developing nation: A nation that does not have the social or physical infrastructure necessary to provide a modern standard of living to its middle- and working-class population.

Diaspora: The members of a community that spread out into the wider world, sometimes assimilating to new cultures and sometimes retaining most or all of their original culture.

Diktat: An order from an authority given without popular approval.

Disenfranchise: To take away someone's rights.

Displaced persons: Persons who are forced to leave their home country or a region of their country due to war, persecution, or natural disasters.

Economic boom: A period of rapid economic and financial growth, resulting in greater wealth and more purchasing power.

Economic reserves: Currency, usually in the form of gold, used to support the paper money distributed through an economy, available to be used by a government when its own currency does not have enough value.

Edict: A proclamation by a person in authority that functions the same as a law.

Embargo: An official ban on trade.

Federation: A country formed by separate states with a central government that manages national and international affairs, but control over local matters is retained by individual states.

Series Glossary of Key Terms

Food insecurity: Being without reliable access to nutritious food at an affordable price and in sufficient quantity.

Free-floating currency: A currency whose value is determined by the free market, changing according to supply and demand for that currency.

Fundamentalist: A political and/or religious ideology based explicitly on traditional orthodox concepts, with rejection of modern values.

Gross Domestic Product (GDP): The total value of goods and services a country produces in a given time frame.

Hegemony: Dominance of one nation over others.

Heretical: When someone's beliefs contradict an orthodox religion.

Indigenous: Referring to a person or group native to a particular place.

Industrialization: The transition from an agricultural economy to a manufacturing economy.

Inflation: A general increase in prices and a decrease in the purchasing value of money.

Insurgency: An organized movement aimed at overthrowing or destroying a government.

Islamist: A military or political organization that believes in the fundamentals of Islam as the guiding principle, rather than secular law; often used synonymously (although not always accurately) with Islamic terrorism.

Jihad: A struggle or exertion on behalf of Islam, sometimes through armed conflict.

Judiciary: A network of courts within a society and their relationship to each other.

Mercantilism: A historical economic theory that focuses on the trade of raw materials from a colony to the mother country, and of manufactured goods from the mother country to the colony, for the profit of the mother country.

Migrant: A person who moves from place to place, either by choice or due to warfare or other economic, political, or environmental crises.

Militia: A group of volunteer soldiers who do not fight with a military full-time.

Municipal elections: Elections held for office on the local level, such as town, city, or county.

Nationalize: When an industry or sector of the economy is totally owned and operated by the government.

Parliamentary: Governmental structure in which executive power is awarded to a cabinet of legislative body members, rather than elected by the people directly.

Paramilitary: Semimilitarized force, trained in tactics and organized by rank, but not officially part of a nation's formal military.

Patriarchy: A system of society or government in which power is held by men.

Police state: Nation in which the state closely monitors activity and harshly punishes any citizen thought to be critical of society or the government.

Populism: An approach to politics, often with authoritarian elements, that emphasizes the role of ordinary people in a society's government over that of an elite class.

Propagandist: A person who disseminates government-created communications, like TV shows and posters, that seek to directly influence and control a national audience to serve the needs of the government, sometimes employing outright falsehoods.

Proportional representation: An electoral system in which political parties gain seats in proportion to the number of votes cast for those seats.

Protectionist: Actions on behalf of a government to stem international trade in favor of helping domestic businesses and producers.

Reactionary: A person who opposes new social and economic ideas or reforms; a person who seeks a return to past forms of governance.

Referendum: A decision on a particular issue put up to a popular vote.

Refugee: A person who leaves his or her home nation, by force or by choice, to flee from war or oppression.

Reparations: Payments made to someone to make amends for wrongdoing.

Republicanism: A political philosophy of representative government in which citizens elect leaders to govern.

Rubber-stamp legislature: Legislative body with formal authority but little, if any, decision-making power and subordinate to another branch of government or political party leadership.

Sanctions: Political and/or economic punishments levied against another nation as punishment for wrongdoing.

Secretariat: A permanent administrative office or department, usually in government, and the staff of that office or department.

Sect: A subgroup of a major religion, with individual beliefs or philosophies that divide it from other subgroups of the religion.

Series Glossary of Key Terms

Sovereignty: The ability of a country to rule itself.

Statute: A law created and passed by a legislative body.

Subsidies: Amounts of money that a government gives to a particular industry to help manage prices or promote social or economic policies.

Tariff: A tax or fee placed on imported or exported products.

Theocratic: Of or relating to a theocracy, a form of government that lays claim to God as the source and justification of its authority.

Totalitarian: A form of government where power is in the hands of a single person or group.

Trade deficit: The degree to which a country must buy more imports than it sells exports; can reflect economic problems as well as strong buying power.

Trade surplus: The degree to which a country can sell more exports than it purchases; can reflect economic strength as well as poor buying power.

Welfare state: A system where the government publically funds programs to ensure the health and well-being of its citizens.

Chronology of Key Events

2333 BCE	Legendary founding of Korean kingdom and official starting date of Korean history.
108 BCE	China's Han Dynasty destroys Korea's kingdom, separating it into four districts and bringing Korea into China's sphere of influence.
372	Buddhism arrives in Korea.
676	Defeat of Chinese military and reunification of three kingdoms of Korea into one state.
1033	Korea builds massive wall along northern border, akin to China's great wall.
1231	Mongol invasion of Korea; the Mongols would rule Korea (and almost all of East Asia) for the next century.
1598	Korea defeats Japanese military invasion.
1653	Dutch captain Hendrick Hamel, perhaps the first European to reach Korea, shipwrecked on Jeju Island.
1873	Korean ports opened to Western trade.
1905	Korea becomes Japanese colony after Japan's victory in the Russo-Japanese War; harsh treatment by the Japanese for the next 40 years leads to freedom movements such as Kim Il-sung's.
1945	Japan is defeated in World War II, and Korea is placed into two zones of control: the United States in the south, and the Soviet Union in the north.
1950	The Korean War begins as Kim Il-sung, supported by the Communist Soviet Union, invades the south.
1953	Korean War ends in armistice (but not a formal peace treaty).
1960	Protests overthrow the corrupt First Republic of South Korea.
1966	Fear of China's Cultural Revolution leads to mass migration over the North Korean border.
1968	Unsuccessful assassination attempt by North Korea on South Korea's president Park Chung-hee.
1979	South Korean intelligence operatives assassinate Park Chung-hee.

1987	A major pro-democracy movement overthrows the military dictatorship of South Korea; the country transitions into public elections and transparency.
1991	The USSR collapses, ending a period of economic aid and relative prosperity in North Korea.
1994	Kim Il-sung dies and his son, Kim Jong-il, takes power; start of the North Korean famine.
1998	North Korea tests first long-range missile.
2006	North Korea tests a nuclear weapon.
2010	Naval and artillery exchanges between North and South Korea result in dozens killed, but no further action taken by either side.
2011	Kim Jong-il dies and Kim Jong-un takes power, beginning a series of purges and crackdowns to cement his authority, including executing his own uncle.
2018	Kim Jong-un meets U.S. President Donald Trump at a summit in Singapore, the first meeting between a U.S. president and a leader of North Korea.

Further Reading & Internet Resources

Books

De Mente, Boye Lafayette. *The Korean Mind: Understanding Contemporary Issues*. Clarendon, VT: Tuttle Publishing, 2018. This new work helps outsiders to better understand the Korean psyche across both sides of the border, providing unique views of everyday Korean life.

Demick, Barbara. *Nothing to Envy: Ordinary Lives in North Korea*. New York: Spiegel & Grau, 2010. With interviews from over 100 different North Korean refugees, Demick (a former bureau chief in Beijing) details the everyday and the extraordinary in North Korea.

Hong, Euny. *The Birth of Korean Cool: How One Nation Is Conquering the World through Pop Culture*. London: Picador Publishing, 2014. This Korean immigrant's story of how South Korea is punching above its weight is a unique and refreshing look at Korean culture.

Hwang, Kyung Moon. *A History of Korea*. London: Palgrave Macmillan, 2016. Covering the mythical founding of Korea up until the modern day, this is one of the most comprehensive works of Korean history available to read.

Oberdorfer, Don. *The Two Koreas: A Contemporary History*. New York: Basic Books, 2013. Looking at the schism between North and South Korea, Oberdorfer analyzes the strikingly different paths that both nations have taken since the end of the Korean War.

Tudor, Daniel. *Korea: The Impossible Country*. Clarendon, VT: Tuttle Publishing, 2012. A look at the economic miracle pulled off by South Korea, raising its entire country from a relative backwater into a global leader of capitalism.

Web Sites

38 North. *http://www.38north.org*

Asia Society. *https://asiasociety.org/education/korean-history-and-political-geography*

Korean Central News Agency. *https://kcnawatch.co*

Korea.net. *http://www.korea.net*

Korea News. *New York Times*. *https://www.nytimes.com/topic/destination/south-korea*

The Korean War: U.S. Army Overview. *https://www.army.mil/koreanwar/*

Index

A
abortion, 82
abuses, 28–30, 42–43, 63
age distribution, 87, 89
aggressions, 14, 20–22
   See also conflicts; wars
agriculture, 6, 11, 14, 51, 56–60, 62, 68, 100
alliances, 9, 26–27, 39
Americans, 94
Amrok River, 11
assassinations, 32, 105
Australia, 28
automobiles, 27, 60–62

B
banking, 52–54
Bareunmirae Party (South), 43
biases, 82, 88
black market, 52, 56, 68
Buddhism, 87, 91–93, 105
Bush, George W., 33

C
Canada, 28
capital punishment, 34, 39, 42, 76, 80
   See also executions
capitalism, 7, 13, 20
Catholicism, 81–82, 87, 93
cell phones, 67, 76
Central Bank (North), 53
Central Intelligence Agency (CIA), 22, 55
Central Military Commission (North), 46–47
children, 12, 75, 86–90
China, 6, 8, 10–11, 13, 15, 20–22, 26–30, 47, 63
Chinese, 94
Chinese (language), 95
Christianity, 81–82, 87, 91, 93, 97
cities, 10–11, 14
climate, 6, 70, 77
Clinton, Hillary, 23
coal, 6, 14, 62, 64
Cold War, 7–8, 18, 22, 53
   See also containment
communism, 7–8, 14–15, 18, 20, 22, 34–36, 39, 80, 97, 100
   See also containment; governments; politics
conflicts, 7–9, 11, 14, 20–22, 26–27, 105
Confucianism, 87, 91, 93
containment, 18, 20
contraception, 66–67, 82
copper, 6, 62
corruption, 36, 44–46, 68
counterfeiting, 63
courts, 42, 47–49
criminality, 73–74
cultures, 11–13, 28, 53–54, 82–83, 86–97
currencies, 51–52

D
danil minjok, 94
   See also Juche ideology
Day of the Sun, 97–98
defectors, 28–29, 34, 43, 60, 75, 101
deforestation, 77
demilitarized zone (DMZ), 13–14, 18, 22, 95
democracy, 7, 12, 18, 20, 34, 36, 47, 80–81
   See also governments; politics
Democratic Front for the Reunification of the Fatherland (North), 43
Democratic Party of Korea (South), 43
demographics, 6, 12, 14, 30, 56, 66–70, 82–83, 86–96
denuclearization, 24–26, 31
diaspora, 86, 96, 101
dictatorship, 20, 34–36, 46–47, 80–81
diet, 57–58, 68–69, 96–97
   See also foods
discrimination, 81–82, 94–95
   See also danil minjok; Juche ideology
disease, 68–70, 77
dissent, 13, 74
   See also protests
drug trafficking, 30–31

E
economies, 15, 27–28, 50–64, 72, 78–80
education, 28, 53–54, 67, 74–75, 84
elderly, 88–90
elections, 12, 36, 43–44, 47, 81
electricity, 67, 70–71, 78
E-Mart Traders, 69
embargoes, 13, 101
energy, 14, 64, 67, 71, 77–78
English (language), 95
environment, 77
espionage, 22, 32
ethnic groups, 87, 94
executions, 28–29, 34, 39, 42–43, 74, 80
executive branch (South), 36, 38, 44–47
exports, 14, 51, 58, 62–63

F
famine, 56, 60, 68
fauna, 77
fertility rate, 12, 67, 82, 86–90
foods, 57–58, 60, 68–69, 96–97
foreign relations, 27–31
forests, 6, 77
freedoms, 10, 12, 34–36, 38–39, 80–81

G
Gates, Robert M., 23
gender imbalance, 29, 82
geography, 6, 11, 14, 58–59
Global Gender Gap Report, 82
Goguryeo Baekje Kingdom, 8, 15
governments, 7, 34–48
graphite, 14

108 Nations in the News: THE KOREAS

gross domestic product (Nouth), 69
gross domestic product (South), 58, 69
Group of Twenty (G20), 28
Gwangbokjeol, 39–40, 97

H
Hallasan, 11
Hamhung, 15
Han River, 11
happiness, 74
health care, 68–70, 77, 86, 89–90
heroin, 30
Hezbollah, 33
history, 7–8, 15, 20, 39–40, 91–93, 105–106
holidays, 35, 39–41, 87, 97–98
homosexuality, 81–82
housing, 71–73
Human Freedom Index, 80
human rights, 28–30
human trafficking, 29–30
Hyundai, 27, 50, 60

I
illegal drugs, 30–31
immigration, 88–89, 94
imports, 51, 62–64, 68–69
imprisonment, 10, 28–29, 74, 76, 80
Incheon, 15
independence, 35, 39
India, 28
indoctrination, 7, 10, 74–75
industry, 18, 51, 60–62, 77
inequality, 12, 56, 78, 80–82
inflation, 51–52, 102
infrastructure, 68–72
International Worker's Day, 87
Internet access, 10, 12, 67, 76
invasions, 20–21
Iran, 27, 33
iron, 6, 14

J
Japan, 8–11, 14, 24, 26–27, 39, 50, 105
Japanese, 95
Japanese (language), 95
Jeju dialect, 95

Jeju Island, 11, 105
Jenkins, Charles Robert, 95
Jeonse, 72
Joseon Dynasty, 93
Juche ideology, 37–38, 82, 95, 97
  See also danil minjok
judicial branch (North), 49
judicial branch (South), 36, 42, 47–48
Justice Party (South), 43

K
kidnapping, 22, 95
Kim cult, 74–75, 80, 90, 93–94, 97
Kim dynasty. *See individual Kim members*
Kim Il-sung, 6, 10, 15, 20–22, 32, 37, 54, 78, 80, 97
Kim Jong-il, 10, 15, 17, 37
Kim Jong-un, 9–10, 14–15, 22, 24, 26, 32, 37, 39, 46–47, 55–56
kimchi, 57–58, 96
Korean Bay, 6
Korean People's Army (North), 19, 30
Korean War, 7–8, 17, 20–22, 75, 78, 80, 105
K-pop music, 13
Kumsusan Memorial Palace of the Sun, 15

L
labor forces, 51, 53–60, 82, 89–90
languages, 7, 12–13, 87, 94–96
  See also Jeju dialect; Pyongyang dialect
lead, 6
Lee Myung-bak, 78–79
legal systems, 34–43
legislative branch (South), 36, 38, 47
Liberation Day, 39–41, 97
Liberty Korea Party (South), 43
Libya, 27
life expectancy, 56, 67–68, 77, 90
limestone, 6
literacy, 74–75

M
malnutrition, 68–69, 96
Manwoldae Palace, 15
Mao Zedong, 20–21
markets, 58, 60
marriage, 40–41, 81, 88
media, 10, 67, 76
medical care, 68–70, 77, 86, 89–90
methamphetamines, 30, 63
militaries, 6, 8, 19, 26, 30–33, 46–47, 61
minerals, 62
Ministry of Unification (South Korea), 13
Minjung Party (South), 43
miscegenation, 66, 82, 88–89, 94–95
  See also danil minjok; Juche ideology
missiles, 9, 17, 22, 106
molybdenum, 6
Mongolia, 29
Moon Jae-in, 24–25, 46
mortality rate, 67, 70, 90

N
narcotics, 30–31
National Assembly (South), 43, 47
National Health Insurance, 69
natural resources, 6, 14, 62–64
North Korean Communist Party, 36, 39, 43, 46
North Korean Constitution, 9–10, 31, 35, 39
Nuclear Non-Proliferation Treaty, 10, 31
nuclear weapons, 9–10, 14, 17, 22–23, 26–27, 31, 106
  See also denuclearization
nutrition, 68–69, 90, 96

O
obesity, 67
oil, 27, 62, 64
Olympics, 25, 28
opportunities, 78–80
Organization for Economic Co-operation and Development (OECD), 53, 56, 69

Index 109

P

Paris Agreement, 78
Park Geun-hye, 44–46, 80
parliament, 38
political parties, 34, 43, 46–47
politics, 34–48, 52
pollution, 77–78
population, 6, 14, 30, 86–89
poverty, 13, 30, 50, 56–57, 67–71, 78, 96
prayer ribbons, 13
precious metals, 6
president, 38, 44–47, 78–79
prime minister, 44, 46
prostitution, 29–30, 81
Protestantism, 87
protests, 45, 80
  See also dissent
Pyongyang, 10, 14–15, 77–78, 82
Pyongyang dialect, 95

Q

QR Video
  end of the Korean war, 25
  Juche ideology, 37
  life in a South Korean city, 16
  a North Korean home, 73
  North Korean *Jangmadan*, 60
  traditional religious ritual, 93

R

racism, 82, 88, 94–95
  See also *Juche* ideology
recent news, 17
refugees, 18, 28–29, 93–95
religion, 11, 13, 38, 81–82, 87, 91–93, 97, 105
  See also Kim cult
repression, 7, 10, 29, 34, 76, 80
Republic of Korea Air Force (South), 19
Republic of Korea Army (South), 19
Republic of Korea Navy (South), 19
reunification, 13, 25–26, 43, 46

rights, 10, 34–36, 38–40, 49, 80–81
rogue nations, 27
Russia, 10–11, 26, 29

S

sabotage, 22
safety, 73–74
Samsung, 15, 27, 50, 60, 76
sanctions, 7, 10, 13, 26, 31, 103
sanitation, 67, 70–71
Sea of Japan, 6
Seoraksan National Park, 11
Seoul, 11, 14–15, 72–73
Seoul dialect, 95
sex ratio, 82, 87
sex trade, 29–30
  See also human trafficking
shamanism, 93
shindo, 93
Sikhism, 93
Silla Kingdom, 8
Singapore, 28, 106
slavery, 29–30, 55
smoking, 77, 90–91
smuggling, 11, 30, 56, 93
social mobility, 78–80
socialism, 39, 55
songbun ideology, 78, 80, 82
South Korean Constitution, 35, 38, 48
Soviet Union, 8, 20–21, 26, 49, 105–106
spending, 19, 32
sports, 25, 28
subsidies, 56, 66, 69, 72, 104
suicide, 54, 75
summits, 24–26, 106
Supreme Court (North), 49
Supreme Court (South), 42, 47–48
Supreme People's Assembly (North), 47
Syngman Rhee, 20–21

T

technology, 60–61, 76
Ten Principles, 39
terrorism, 32–33
Thais, 94
threats, 17, 22–24
tolerance, 82

torture, 28, 42
trade, 13, 27–28, 32–33, 62–63
  See also economies
Trump, Donald, 17, 24, 26, 33, 106
tungsten, 6, 14

U

unemployment, 51, 53–55, 58, 73–74
United Nations (UN), 13, 22, 28, 62
United States (US), 8–10, 20, 22–24, 26, 30–32, 105
  See also containment
universities, 84
urban areas, 6, 15, 72–73, 77–78, 82
  See also Pyongyang; Seoul

V

Victory Day, 23
Vietnam, 29
Vietnam War, 22
Vietnamese, 94
violence, 73–74
voting, 12, 36, 38, 43–44, 47, 81

W

Warmbier, Otto, 42
wars, 7, 20–22, 75, 78, 80, 105
water, 11, 67, 70–71
weddings, 40–41
Winter Olympics (2018), 25
women, 12, 29, 66–68, 80, 82–83, 86–88
won, 51–53
Worker's Party of Korea, 46
World Bank, 13
World Cup, 28
World Economic Forum, 82
World War II, 20, 27, 37, 39, 105

Y

Yalu River, 21, 57
yellow dust, 77
Yeonpyeong Island, 22
youths, 12–13, 54–55, 72–75, 84, 88–90, 95

Z

zinc, 6

Author's Biography

David Wilson has a bachelor's degree in history from Miami University and a graduate degree in history from the University of Cincinnati. His writings on history have been published by educational institutes like Norwich University, Peregrine Academics, and Study.com. He lives in Denver.

Credits

Cover

Top (left to right): gkgraphics/iStock; Mienny/iStock; http://www.president.go.kr/Wikimedia Commons
Middle (left to right): momcilog/iStock; Viktoriagam/Dreamstime; Presse750/Dreamstime
Bottom (left to right): Eric Broder Van Dyke/Shutterstock; narvikk/iStock; Alexey Novikov/Dreamstime

Interior

1, Leonard Zhukovsky/Shutterstock; 6, Astrelok/Shutterstock; 8, Tata Donets/Shutterstock; 9, Cmglee/Wikimedia Commons; 11, Perati Komson/Shutterstock; 12, Yeongsik Im/Shutterstock; 13, UnknownLatitude Images/Shutterstock; 15, Truba7113/Shutterstock; 19, Christophe BOISSON/Shutterstock; 21 (UP LE), Hulton Archive/Getty Images/Wikimedia Commons; 21 (UP RT), Wikimedia Commons; 21 (LO LE), Wikimedia Commons; 21 (LO RT), Foreign Languages Edition, Pyongyang/Wikimedia Commons; 23 (LO), Stefan Krasowski/Wikimedia Commons; 24, Hadrian/Shutterstock; 25, Leonard Zhukovsky/Shutterstock; 32, Astrelok/Shutterstock; 35, Sagase48/Shutterstock; 36, Yeongsik Im/Shutterstock; 37, Astrelok/Shutterstock; 38, Rheo1905/Wikimedia Commons; 40, YCPMKK Gallery/Shutterstock; 41, Freda Bouskoutas/iStock; 42, Tom Uhlman/Polaris/Newscom; 44, Frederic Legrand - COMEO/Shutterstock; 45 (UP), Sagase48/Shutterstock; 45 (LO), Byungsuk Ko/Shutterstock; 46, Sagase48/Shutterstock; 48, Nudimmud/Wikimedia Commons; 51, Yonhap News/YNA/Newscom; 52, The Bank of Korea/Wikimedia Commons; 54, Anton_Ivanov/Shutterstock; 55, Attila JANDI/Shutterstock; 57 (UP), Stefan Bruder/Shutterstock; 57 (LO), 365FOOD/Shutterstock; 58, Roman Babakin/Shutterstock; 59, FrankRamspott/iStock; 61, SarahTz/Wikimedia Commons; 67, Gina Smith/Shutterstock; 69, Sorbis/Shutterstock; 70, Sanga Park/Shutterstock; 73, amnat30/Shutterstock; 75, amnat30/Shutterstock; 76, Tom Gowanlock/Shutterstock; 78, TTLSC/Shutterstock; 79, hojusaram from Seoul/Wikimedia Commons; 81, Sungmin Cho/Shutterstock; 83, chaelinjane/Shutterstock; 84, qingqing/Shutterstock; 87, Anton_Ivanov/Shutterstock; 88, Mikhail Priakhin/Shutterstock; 89, Niyazz/Shutterstock; 90, Roman Harak - North Korea/Wikimedia Commons; 91, Yeongsik Im/Shutterstock; 92, MicheleB/Shutterstock; 94, Chintung Lee/Shutterstock; 97, Johnathan21/Shutterstock; 98 (UP), artistVMG/Shutterstock; 98 (LO), Uri Tours/Wikimedia Commons